Milly and the Tale from Across the Street

A Milly Story

by Martha Langager Klopp

Odin's Opus

Odin's Opus Publishing

ISBN: 978-1-7332089-1-8

Thanks, Jon, for your guidance in story-telling.

For my family: my husband, Dan, and my children, Sofia, Madeline, Josie, and Will; and of course our dogs, Odin and Ginny

Chapter 1

*M*illy had a habit of spying on that beautiful, old, yellow house across their quiet street in St. Paul, Minnesota. She couldn't help it; the house was super old, but so grand compared to her own modern, practical home. She secretly hoped to see ghosts in the window. Maybe she just wanted to catch glimpses of the adorable cat that slipped in and out.

She never expected to see *that*, though. Not even in her wildest dreams.

It was a year ago. Last summer she saw something that she would think back on every day, and she hasn't seen it happen again since. The old man who lived there had been standing on his front porch carrying his cat. He looked like he was having a deep conversation with it. Then, all of a sudden Milly saw the old man abruptly look around the neighborhood and suddenly take off into the air, still holding the cat. Flying. He didn't have a rocket, wings, balloons... nothing. He was just up in the air and rose up until he was as high as an eagle. Just as quickly as it started, he sped off into the distance, still in the air.

The only person Milly told was Tommy, her older brother. Tommy's reaction was hard to read. He had put on a show for her; he pretended to think it was cool, but she could tell he was just trying to be nice. Exactly how you would act when a little two year old tells you he wants to be a helicopter when he grows up.

That was the old, twelve year old Tommy. He was nice to Milly and did anything for her, even believing wild stories about the neighbor or playing make believe. Now, Tommy was turning into a teenager, and with that came crabby moods and "too cool" attitudes. The only time he spoke to Milly anymore was to shush her while he was on the phone or to make fun of her.

Milly especially missed the old Tommy because she didn't have many friends. Her best friends were from her soccer team, but they all went to different schools than her. At school, a lot of the girls were already into shopping and makeup, while Milly still wanted to run around at the playground. She knew she didn't want to change who she was just to not be so lonely.

***

Milly lounged on the couch, cuddling with her family's yellow lab, Angus. She stared at the old, yellow house, lost in thought over last year's flying man incident, when a moving truck suddenly pulled up. Was the old man moving out? The last time she saw him was probably half a year ago. Nobody was bringing stuff out of the house, rather people were unloading from the truck into the house.

"There's a moving truck outside that one house across the street! Is someone moving in?" Milly said to her mom across the room. "Oh! Really? I don't know. This would be news to me. That man kept to himself, so I'm not sure. That would be pretty neat if a family with kids moved in, huh? Come on, you haven't eaten breakfast yet," Milly's mom said as she motioned towards the kitchen. Milly could have closed her eyes and let the pleasant smell of french toast lead her.

As Milly poured her maple syrup, she let herself get lost in the fantasy of a new best friend moving in across the street. She was fairly certain there would be a family with kids, including a ten year old girl. They would get ice cream cones, run around at the playground, read books together, go on adventures… and of course, explore that beautiful, old, yellow house.

Bonus would be if that family had a cat! Milly loved Angus, but she had always wanted a cat. They were never able to get one because of her dad's allergy. Milly was sure her new friend would appreciate

Angus just as much as she would appreciate the cat. Why not throw in an older boy who could be friends with Tommy. He could use a friend who wanted to do something other than play video games or be grumpy all day.

The timing was perfect, as summer vacation was in full swing. Milly couldn't wait!

Milly gobbled her last bite of french toast and quickly washed it down with orange juice. Her mom took a slow sip of her steamy coffee and smiled with her eyes. "What do you think? Want to help make muffins to bring over to the new neighbors?" she slyly asked. Milly smiled brightly.

***

Heavenly was a good word to describe the smell of the muffins. The blueberries were wild, from last summer's gathering at her grandparents' cabin.

Milly suggested she and Tommy could split a warm muffin "just to make sure they're good". Milly's mom obliged and split up a couple muffins between the three of them. Milly agreed they would be a nice welcoming gift.

"Coming, Tommy?" Milly's mom asked.

"No," Tommy mumbled thoughtlessly.

With a straw basket in hand, Milly's mom led Milly across the street. Milly felt butterflies in her stomach.

Milly's mom pushed the doorbell but there was no ding whatsoever. After another try with no result, she sighed and delicately rapped on the heavy door. Seconds later Milly knocked quite a bit more boldly as her mom's knock was much too polite. Milly heard footsteps approaching the door followed by the loud creak. A tall, jovial looking man in his forties stood there.

"Hello, we're your new neighbors," Milly's mom said, motioning across the road. "My name is Dorothy Hagen, and this is my daughter Milly. Here's a little treat to welcome you! Where are you hailing from?"

"Oh, hello! Great to meet some neighbors. That was quick, alright! We just arrived bright and early this morning from Willmar out in western Minnesota. My name is Doug Nelson. You gotta meet my wife and daughters, hold on," the man rapidly exclaimed. Then he yelled back over his shoulder, "Rachel! Cora! Evie! Come meet the neighbors!" Milly tried to peek past Mr. Nelson but she couldn't see much of anything besides big cardboard boxes.

The two girls appeared after only half a minute and the mother joined soon after, and said "Wow, hello there. I'm Rachel, nice to meet you!"

The Hagens introduced themselves again, and Milly learned the girl her age was Cora while the older one was Evie.

"I've never heard the name Milly before. Interesting. Do you have any brothers or sisters?" Evie asked warily.

"I have an older brother Tommy," replied Milly, "and my name *is* kind of different. I wish my mom named me something normal." Milly felt the familiar sting of rejection.

Evie shrugged her shoulders and said, "Hope to meet Tommy later. I need to get back to unpacking my room."

"I think Milly is a cool name!" Cora assured Milly. "Do you go to Martin Cove Middle School?" Cora added hopefully.

"Yeah, about to start my first year there! You?" Milly felt a surge of excitement.

"Yeah! I'm glad I'll have a friend there," Cora said in relief. All Milly could do was smile.

CHAPTER 1½

He was in a sour mood. He knew he needed help if his plan was going to work. Chester said he would call the police if he bothered him again. He just needs time to simmer down and he would be compliant after that. Chester couldn't just ignore him forever.

He knew patience was important, but it was becoming unbearable to live in a world with whiny, obnoxious brats. He was never that awful, even as a kid. There was no way he would waste time with frivolous pursuits like they do. The plan needed to start as soon as possible.

Chapter 2

A couple days later, Milly finally got the anticipated invitation to the beautiful, old, yellow house. She could barely contain her excitement that morning.

"I'm going to Cora's house now," Milly said casually. "I get to see the house. You jealous?" Milly made her eyebrows jump up and down.

"Actually, yes," her mom replied stoically.

"Yup. Me too. Not going to lie!" her dad laughed. "Will you be back for lunch?"

"I hope not! I can call you later and let you know!" Milly yelled over her shoulder as she walked to the door.

After closing the front door and looking for cars, Milly sprinted across the street. The lions in the front yard of the big yellow house seemed to eye her suspiciously. Milly rapped on the front door and stood there patiently.

"Hey! I'm excited to finally have a friend over to my new house! My room is sweet, let's go see that first!" Cora exclaimed. Milly knew the mysteries would probably not be in Cora's bedroom but she'd see the rest of the house eventually. The foyer was grand: tall ceilings, dark and ornate wood and a front and center staircase. Milly and Cora bounded up the squeaky stairs.

"My parents, Chester, and I have our rooms on this floor but Evie got the third floor, of course. She gets to be on the same floor as the tower," Cora said as she pointed up the second set of stairs.

"Chester?" Milly asked curiously.

"Yeah, he's my great-great-uncle. That's why we moved in... we're apparently his closest family and he needed help. Betsy, my great-great aunt died years back, no kids... He didn't want to move into a nursing home, but he's basically bed-ridden now," Cora explained.

Milly hadn't realized Cora was related to the flying man! Milly wondered whether Cora had any idea about that side of Chester or whether she should even say anything. Now that a year had gone by, she was starting to question whether it really happened or not.

Cora's room was very tidy. The walls were plastered with faded wallpaper in a peacock design and there was a nice bay window, already with a new cushion: the perfect place to read or watch out the window. There was a small attached bathroom complete with a fancy clawfoot bath. Cora's canopy four poster bed fit in with the Victorian style, along with her desk. "The first day we were here we did some antique shopping," Cora said. "Come on, I'll show you the rest of the house!"

"That's Chester's room. I'm sure he's sleeping," Cora said as they passed by a bedroom. Down the hall they peeked into her parent's bedroom, which had its own attached bathroom as well. There was a maid service pull chord on one of the walls. Milly envisioned the first owners of the house strolling across the spacious bedroom and summoning the maid for tea.

Cora led Milly up the second set of stairs where they encountered Evie's bedroom with short, sloping ceilings. A hallway brought them to the turret. The windows made the top floor bright and inviting. "I'm not sure what the tower is for," Cora said, shrugging her shoulders.

A flash of orange and white darted from Evie's bedroom and down the stairs causing Milly to let out a gasp.

"Oh. That was Patty. I hope you weren't expecting to actually pet her. She only likes Evie and Chester. She's probably bumming because Evie went out for a run."

The rest of the house was begging to be explored, so they made their way to the first floor again. The kitchen was bright and cheerful and it had an attached pantry and a fancy dining room beyond that. The next room they entered was a library that was just as breathtaking as the grand foyer. On the other side of the foyer was a formal living room. The walls were updated to muted greens and neutral shades.

"I'll show you the basement now," Cora said, already on her way down the set of stairs near the kitchen. The basement had a treadmill and weight lifting bench, plus piles of boxes covering the old thin carpet. Milly followed Cora, weaving through the mess, until they made their way to the laundry room. Milly tried to scour every inch with her eyes, desperate to find something cool.

"Don't tell my parents I brought you down here…" Cora said seriously.

Milly's heart missed a beat. *Is she about to lead me to a family secret? A treasure box? Is this where the ghosts live?!*

"It is SUCH a mess down here and my mom doesn't want anyone to see. I think it is just basically old toys and a bunch of junk they didn't have time to figure out what to do with. I hope they just cart it off to Goodwill!" Cora added.

Oh. The family secret is a mess! Milly reassured herself that the tour wasn't incredibly thorough and there could be room for surprises still.

As soon as they were in the kitchen again, Cora's mom popped her head from the hallway and chirped "Oh hello, Milly! So good to see you again!"

Milly let out a comically loud gasp and Cora doubled over laughing.

"Jumpy much?" Cora said between giggles. Milly smirked and realized she *was* a little tightly wound at the moment.

"Good to see you too," Milly finally responded.

The library seemed to draw Milly and Cora back. The door was wide open, inviting them in. "My parents think these books have been on the bookcases from before my great-great-uncle was here. I've never heard of any of them," Cora said as she led her fingers along the spines of several bound books.

Milly pulled one out that was bound in dark brown leather and opened it gently. The pages were thin. When she placed it back, a navy colored book caught her eye because it was taller and thinner than the rest, plus there was not a single word on its spine. She went to pull it out, but the book wouldn't budge, further piquing her interest. "Oh, I don't want to break this book, but why won't it come out?"

"Huh. Just yank it," Cora said. Milly was just waiting for those words and gave the book a pull but still nothing. She changed her grip to the top of the book, looking for a tighter grip. She yanked again and the book finally released from the bookcase. The book was not a book at all, but a lookalike that opened as a box. Milly opened it and the girls stared into the disappointing void. You couldn't even make out a dust molecule, let alone a secret stash of something. Milly sighed and was just about to return the book, when Cora yelled, "Wait!"

Chapter 3

Cora pointed to the back of the bookcase where the navy book had been. A single, unassuming key was just sitting there.

"Get it!" Milly urged.

Cora slowly grasped the key, then whipped it out like a snake was about to strike. The key was small and very old looking. Milly whispered, "Can I hold it?"

Cora handed it to her and Milly flipped it around, looking for any kind of label: words, symbols, numbers, anything to give a clue of its purpose, but there was nothing. "What does this key do?" Milly asked rhetorically. "Let's try it on the front door," Milly finally suggested.

Milly tip-toed to the front door. She carefully wiggled the key into the old lock, but it was clear it wasn't going to fit. She made her way back in the house and the two girls plopped on the couch in the library.

"OK, this would be so incredibly way too cool, but do you think there's a secret room in here that the key opens? I've always wanted a secret room in my house," Milly pondered.

"That would be so cool," Cora said as she sprang up off the couch and started investigating the walls of the library. Milly joined her excitedly. Her heart was pounding, but a secret room was too perfect to hope for.

Milly ran her fingers along the whole bookcase, her eyes scanning up and down. At the end of the bookcase, there was a lamp that was affixed to the wall. She had noticed that almost everything, especially on the main floor, was updated. New lamps, new appliances, and new flooring. This lamp was oddly antiquated: an antique, but one that was not beautiful enough to still use. Maybe there was a purpose to this lamp besides lighting. Milly studied every inch of the lamp, until she noticed there was a small latch at the base of the light fixture. She flipped it open and immediately the light sprang up effortlessly, and underneath was a simple key hole.

Milly slid the key in and, smooth as butter, it turned. Right beneath the keyhole a thin drawer sprang open. She immediately didn't see anything in the drawer, so she opened it further and revealed a folded notecard. She took it and carefully unfolded and smoothed it out. Sprawled across in neat handwriting was, "IVKVZG ZUGVI NV: MVEVI TILD GLL LOW LI GLL HVIRLFH GL KOZB".

"This is complete gibberish! Or is it another language?!" said Cora.

"Geez, I don't know. It's gibberish to me too. Maybe it's in code," Milly pointed out.

The two girls stared at the notecard. Milly's mind was busy trying to figure out what it could mean.

Tommy would probably figure this out instantly. He always solved the "Cryptoquip" in the daily newspaper. She didn't want to ask him for help because then he'd want to know what it was for. Plus, he would come up with a million favors she'd have to do in exchange for his help.

"It's probably left from some kid who wanted to play a practical joke," Cora said finally.

"Really? It's gotta be more than a joke. Why would a kid go to that trouble for a joke?" Milly argued.

"Well, it's working! It's got your attention," Cora pointed out.

"Can I bring it home and just try to work it out on my own, then?" Milly asked.

"I don't care, do what you want!" Cora said.

Milly questioned herself. She didn't want to seem like a gullible dork, but at the same time the note had to mean something.

Chapter 4

Milly sat at the desk in her room and just stared at the random letters on the yellowing notecard. She stared for so long her eyes became unfocused and the letters just looked like dark blobs. It didn't even matter; she had no idea how to crack the code.

Reluctantly, she made her way to the den, where she could see the unmistakable flashing lights of a video game. She stood near Tommy's side, where she was obviously visible in his peripheral vision. The video game music was obnoxiously loud.

"What....do you want?" Tommy said irritably without looking over.

"I have a code for you to break," Milly said loudly, trying to speak over the music. "What's it from?" Tommy demanded.

"Oh, we found it at Cora's house," Milly said nonchalantly.

"Why would I want to solve something for you? What's in it for me?"

"It'd make you feel good to be a kind person?" Milly offered weakly.

"Ha!" was all Tommy said in return.

Milly left to return to her room. What could she say to get Tommy to agree? She looked in her secret candy stash and realized she only had a couple leftover Dum Dum lollipops, nothing that would equal a favor. She sighed and stared at the mysterious paper again. "IVKVZG ZUGVI NV: MVEVI TILD GLL LOW LI GLL HVIRLFH GL KOZB" She knew a handful of words in French, Spanish, and German. There was absolutely no resemblance. Milly wished she had tried to do more "Cryptoquip" puzzles in her lifetime. Usually with those, however, they gave you at least one clue.

Even though dinner was her favorite, BLTs, she was lost in her own thoughts.

"Good day, Milly?" Milly's dad said.

"Uh, yeah. Yeah," Milly said absently. Then, she urgently turned to Tommy and said "How about two Dum Dum suckers?"

Tommy snorted in response. "What?! Do you think I'm two? I'm not bribed by Dum Dums."

"OK, how about I do a chore for you?" Milly offered, knowing that was a far cry from a deal as well.

"Four. Four chores."

"Two?"

"Three, and that's as low as I'll go," Tommy stated, his arms folded over his chest. Milly was actually relieved it was only three chores!

Milly's mom and dad had been shooting glances at Tommy and Milly like they were watching a ping pong match until Milly's mom finally asked, "What is this all about?"

Tommy ignored her, but Milly quickly responded, "Oh, I wanted some insider information about middle school." Milly knew that sounded lame and not believable, but they seemed to buy it.

It was supposed to be Tommy's turn to do the dishes after dinner, but Milly did it without him even asking. Hopefully he would help her with the code after!

After dishes, Milly found Tommy playing video games again and she cleared her throat loudly. "Ready?" she asked hopefully.

"Nah, you gotta do all three chores before I help," he said.

"Fine. One down, then," Milly responded glumly.

"Um, no. You have zero down actually," Tommy retorted snidely.

"I just did the dishes!" Milly squealed.

"I didn't ask you to do them. I thought you just *wanted* to do them since you're such a kind person!"

Tommy was obviously very proud of himself. Milly didn't want to lose out on the help she was going to get so she bottled up her anger.

"OK then, Tommy, what *can* I do for you?"

"I think our bathroom is due for a good scrubbing," Tommy said brightly.

"Oh joy. I'll get on it then."

Cleaning the bathroom was *the* worst chore of all time, but she set to work right away. While Milly was scrubbing the toilet with a brush, Milly's mom popped her head in the bathroom.

"You're really that nervous about starting middle school?" she said, concerned.

"Yeah. I don't have many friends," Milly said sadly, which was kind of true.

"And you think Tommy can really help?"

"Sure!" Milly said. She didn't want to tell her mom about the note they found because she didn't want to get in trouble for snooping around.

After the bathroom was sparkling, Milly knocked on Tommy's room.

"What?!" he barked.

She creaked open the door. "What's next?" she asked, although it was already late and she figured she'd finish the chores the next morning.

"Walk Angus in the morning. And make me breakfast. The works. Sausage, eggs, and pancakes," Tommy said grinning, rubbing his stomach.

"Fine," Milly said quickly.

Perfect, Milly thought. It was a good thing Tommy didn't realize she loved walking Angus and cooking wasn't nearly as bad as cleaning or doing laundry.

Chapter 5

Morning came quicker than normal. She had set her alarm early so she could walk Angus, cook breakfast, and hopefully find out what that message meant. She skipped out the door with Angus wagging his tail in true happiness. Angus loved walks so much that even when members of the family spelled out "walk", he still knew what they were talking about.

Whenever Milly took Angus on their usual mile long route, she always found herself pretending to be on some kind of adventure, whether it was exploring the Amazon rainforest or trekking through the desert in search of water. This time, though, she found herself lost in thought over the key, the message, and the hope for a real secret room. Just like she had seen in the movies.

As she was finishing up her walk, she glanced at Cora's house. Something caught her eye. There was a car parked on the street a couple houses down. That wasn't weird in itself, but Milly recognized it as the same car that she would see frequent the house every couple of months. The car was hard to forget: a shiny black sports car that looked like it belonged in an action movie. Milly shielded her eyes from the sun and squinted. The man inside was writing in a notebook, and he would look up every so often and stare at Cora's house. Milly had an icky feeling in her stomach.

She didn't want him to notice her, so she led Angus in and quickly closed the door behind them. She crept on the couch and peered out at the man again. She saw him glance at his watch, and abruptly turn the car on and peel off. Should she say something to

Cora about him? It was creepy to have someone outside stalking your house.

As she entered the kitchen, her mom was sitting with coffee and lifted her head as she heard Milly enter. "You were up and at 'em early, Milly!" she remarked.

"I walked Angus! Now, I need to make breakfast. Want some eggs, sausage, and pancakes?" she said pleasantly.

"Sure! And I can help!"

She loved cooking with her mom. She never cared when Milly made more of a mess than a meal and she always ate up whatever Milly made, even if it didn't turn out quite right. Milly was whisking eggs when her dad joined them and said, "Breakfast on a Monday? What's the occasion?"

"Why not?" was all Milly said.

**

After cleaning up the kitchen, she barged into Tommy's room. "Time to help me!" she said.

Tommy didn't even look up from his magazine. All he did in response was hold out his hand and motion for her to give him the notecard. Milly silently handed him the mysterious message and crossed her arms and watched him intently. Tommy furrowed his brow and studied the code.

"Are you kidding me? You couldn't figure *this* out?" Tommy guffawed. Milly felt excited and annoyed all at the same time. "This is your basic Reverse Alphabet Code. You're welcome." He flung the notecard towards Milly and returned to his magazine.

As Milly got to her room and slipped into her desk chair, she pondered Reverse Alphabet Code. She had never heard of it before, but guessing from the title alone, she assumed it must mean A equals Z, B equals Y and so on. She should have figured that out on her own, but at this point it was too late to worry about that. She found a piece of scrap paper and wrote out the alphabet, then the reverse alphabet underneath so all the letters were lined up accordingly.

She pulled out the coded message "IVKVZG ZUGVI NV: MVEVI TILD GLL LOW LI GLL HVIRLFH GL KOZB" and got to work changing each letter to their new one. "REPEAT AFTER ME: NEVER GROW TOO OLD OR TOO SERIOUS TO PLAY". Milly smiled pleasantly to herself. It was a nice message, but why was it placed there? Nevertheless, she was excited to show Cora.

Milly got out the front door and yelled over her shoulder, "Going to Cora's! Bye!" Grasping the coded message, she bolted across the street. She knocked without hesitation, and as soon as Cora opened the door, Milly blurted out "Never grow too old or too serious to play!"

Cora stared blankly, utterly confused. "Uh, what?!"

"The coded message says 'Repeat after me: never grow too old or too serious to play!' My brother helped me!" Milly excitedly explained.

"Oh..." Cora slowly replied as she walked into the library, with Milly following her. "So what's the point?" Cora closed the library door soundlessly.

"I don't know!" Milly admitted. "But it's gotta mean something, right?" Milly didn't let Cora's reaction dampen her enthusiasm. Milly strode over to the light fixture that had housed the message.

Cora just stared blankly. "Well, I don't know, it could just be..."

"I know! It's the password. NEVER GROW TOO OLD OR TOO SERIOUS TO PLAY!" Milly interrupted.

The bookcase gave a loud groan and began to shake ever so slightly. Slowly, the bookcase opened up, revealing a room!

Cora and Milly just stared straight ahead into the mysterious room. The newly exposed room was dark and smelled like mothballs. Spider webs were strewn across the door jamb and a dust cloud emerged.

"What is this?" Milly finally asked. "Did you know this was here?"

"No! Does it look like I've seen this before?" Cora asked, giggling. Milly joined in the giggling and the two just stood there in amazement and glee. "What are we waiting for? Let's go in!"

They crept in the room waving their hands around to whip the spider webs out of the way. Just a few feet in the room, the darkness took over and they looked around for lights to turn on. Milly pulled on a cord with no luck.

"I'll have to find some flashlights," Cora said. It was hard to pull away from that room already even if it was just to get flashlights! The two girls backed out and Milly carefully closed the bookcase door. It was heartbreaking to close it. What if they got caught and that was their only chance to explore? Just as Cora creaked open the library door, she saw Cora's mom standing in the doorway of the library, hands on her hips. Milly held her breath.

"Lunch is on the table, girls!" Cora's mom announced.

Phew, she had no idea!

What was on the table for lunch could be cricket sandwiches for all Milly cared. She wolfed down some type of sandwich and gulped her milk. Milly's mind was buzzing. She could not wait to get back in that secret room.

Chapter 6

Cora found a battery powered lantern and a couple flashlights after lunch. They grasped their lights and made their way to the library again and securely closed the door. Milly confidently spoke the password again. Their flashlights stabbed through the darkness, revealing more dust hanging mid-air. Milly's light exposed shelves filled with beakers, canisters, and books. The room itself was about the size of a small bedroom. Along one side of the room, Cora's flashlight shone on a counter with papers scattered about and a leather book, tied loosely with string. Cora set the lantern on the desk and Milly joined her. Cora slowly untied the string and fanned through the pages until she came upon the last page.

September 21, 2018

The risks now outweigh the benefits of my experiments and I may have already caused unintentional consequences. I am not the only one who knows about this room, but I have changed the password. If you are reading this, kudos on solving the riddle, but please just burn this journal _and_ the recipes. I cannot bear to do it myself. I am, however, closing up shop. I cannot be associated with anything in here. There is no need for my side hobby any longer. This is me signing off,

Chester Endicott

"OK, we need to sit down and read this whole journal. Here is our mystery for the summer!" exclaimed Milly.

"For sure," agreed Cora as she turned to the first page. Cora and Milly's eyes were both glued to the notebook.

May 3rd, 1971

We are here! We made it to St. Paul. Compared to Willmar, this feels like the big-time. Because of all my connections at the university, I already have leads on all the top tutors for chemistry at my disposal. If all goes according to plan, Lance will graduate high school early, go to an Ivy League college for undergraduate, and continue on to fulfill our (well, my plans... Betsy thinks I'm going overboard) dreams of another PhD added to the family at a record young age. Did I mention I already got him enrolled at the most prestigious preschool available in the area? Never too early to get the grand plan rolling.

Anyways, this house is beautiful and the secret room is just what I need. It is far more secluded than a basement. I'm only 34 and I think I'm just scratching the surface of what I can

40

accomplish both at the university and my own hobby. I will try to keep up my diary when I need to sort out my thoughts. My ramblings aren't good for much but they do clear my head!

Chester

Milly's stomach fluttered with excitement. *What experiments could Chester have been working on? Were any related to flying?* She hoped the rest of the entries wouldn't be as vague. She simply had to keep reading.

They read silently, pages turning over like a favorite book. Some entries were written quite spaced apart and were bland: rehashing events in the chemistry department, but he also wrote vaguely about his potions every so often.

Milly and Cora read all the way to spring of 1974, when Milly stopped and said, "Before we go on, I'm dying to know what the 'recipes' are and what they do! Let's put a bookmark in and see if we can find the 'recipes'."

Cora nodded and pulled out a gum wrapper she happened to have in her pocket for a makeshift bookmark. On another side of the secret room was another counter spanning the whole length of the wall. There were loose leaf papers haphazardly scattered across it. The two girls collected all the papers. They counted 14 sheets and Cora peered at one and let out a surprised breath.

"Canine Communication. Feline Communication. Rodent Translation. Enhanced Sight. Enhanced Smell. Canine Obedience. Mind Control. Human Flight. Permanent Mood Enhancement. Sleep Aide. Motivation Serum. Memory Enhancement. Dream Manipulation. Human-Animal Conversion," Milly read aloud in amazement.

"Wow, these are intense! I kind of want to try all of them!" Cora exclaimed.

"Me too! Now, I have to tell you something... Last year I saw your uncle Chester talking to Patty in deep conversation and just fly away with her all of a sudden!"

"Why didn't you tell me that sooner!?" Cora squealed.

"I was starting to wonder whether I dreamt it!" Milly said defensively. "But now I know I didn't. This is all just so cool!"

"I probably wouldn't have believed you," admitted Cora.

Milly picked up the first recipe and studied it.

January 1964
Potion for Canine Communication
2 Servings
4th draft

3/4 cup fermented agitemer
1 ½ tablespoons powdered gebrin
2 ¼ teaspoons hilthezern
One pinch turwae

Combine liquid agitemer with gebrin and stir 100 times and let rest for 20 minutes. Meanwhile mix hilthezern and turwae but don't let sit longer *than 5 minutes before you add to agitemer and gebrin mix. Once all four ingredients are in a beaker, you must stir just 10 times and cover overnight a minimum of 10 hours and up to 24 hours roughly. It will lose effectiveness past the 24 hours. Recommended to drink in one quick swoop with low expectations for taste! Results after one hour upon ingestion and expected to last 10 hours.*

"You don't suppose…that this recipe is really real, do you? I mean, if we made this recipe is it possible we could… understand dogs?" Milly said warily, not wanting to sound dumb.

"Seems crazy, but anything is possible. What are these ingredients anyway?" Cora wondered. Milly felt relieved that Cora didn't make fun of her or dismiss the recipe.

Milly and Cora let their eyes scan the room and they laid their eyes on the shelves of containers that ranged from the size of spice containers to much bigger. Milly grasped her flashlight and led them to the shelves.

"Alphabetical order… I see agitemer, both fermented and regular apparently….and a bunch not from that recipe…oh, and here is gebrin and hilthezern. I don't even know if I'm saying those words right. I say let's do this!" Milly exclaimed.

"I would get into so much trouble if we got caught," Cora said softly.

Milly felt a pang of disappointment in her chest. She didn't want to pressure Cora, but she *so* wanted to try out the potion.

She was about to suggest going back to reading the journal, when Cora abruptly exclaimed, "Who cares! Let's just do it!"

The two just looked at each other with big eyes and wide grins.

Bringing over the four ingredients and setting them on the desk seemed to make everything official. Milly quickly located measuring spoons and cups from one of the desk's drawers and opened the fermented agitemer. She almost fell backwards with the sharp smell of the liquid. It was really strong and resembled vinegar and butterscotch.

Milly regained her composure and poured the liquid very slowly into the glass measuring cup until it came up to the ¾ cup line, then she poured it into the beaker. Cora opened the powdered gebrin which surprisingly had no smell, and measured out 1 ½ teaspoons to add in the beaker. Milly held out the wooden spoon which had also been in the drawer and asked "Would you like the honors?"

Cora accepted the spoon and started stirring and counting out loud, "1, 2, 3, 4, 5, 6…." After a couple of minutes, she reached 100 and set the wooden spoon carefully upon the desk.

"We have to wait at least 15 minutes before we can add the other two ingredients," Milly said, glancing at her watch. "It's 1:30. Let's keep reading until it's time!"

The next entry where they left off was another boring entry about chemistry department politics and rants about the parking at the university, but the following entry had an envelope that was attached with a paperclip. The envelope had a return address from "Lance Endicott" in St. Paul, Minnesota, and a Post-It note written in Chester's handwriting had one single word scribbled: "Keep". Endicott sounded vaguely familiar. Milly swore she knew an Endicott, but it was probably some celebrity name or something. Milly opened up the envelope and the two girls read on.

Dear Dad,

Yes, I still want to call you that, even though you want nothing to do with me apparently. I thought you'd be proud of me. I accomplished everything you and mom had expected of me. I thought we'd be on the same page about this. Are you worried I'm going to be too successful in my endeavors? That I will outshine you? Isn't that the purpose of parenthood? To produce offspring that succeeds in life? Let me know if you want to change your mind about our collaboration. The door will always be open for you, being that you are FAMILY.

Sincerely,

Lance

"Yikes! This sounds like some major family drama," Milly noted.

"Well, doesn't every family have some kind of drama?" Cora said defensively.

"I guess," Milly said vaguely. She didn't want to step on any toes and lose a friend. Milly made a mental note not to question Cora's family and felt her confidence in their friendship whither.

Milly looked at her watch and realized it was time for the next step in the recipe. "Let's go mix the last two ingredients!" Milly carefully folded the letter back in the envelope. "OK, once we mix turwae and hilthezern we can't let it sit for more than five minutes! Geez, I've helped my mom bake chocolate chip cookies, banana bread, and some other things, but I have never seen such a strict recipe before!"

Cora nodded her head as she measured out the hilthezern to dump in a smaller container. Milly took a tiny pinch of the turwae and added it. Using a fresh spoon, just in case it mattered, Cora mixed the two ingredients.

"OK, the agimeter and gebrin mixture has been sitting for 19 minutes, so we can add the other two ingredients soon!" Milly said. "What are we going to use to cover the beaker once all four ingredients are together?"

"I don't see lids, I can go find some Saran wrap," offered Cora.

Cora was already out the door before Milly answered. As soon as Cora was gone, Milly realized she was afraid to be alone in the secret room. Milly looked at her watch, which showed 45 seconds until she would need to add the hilthezern and turwae mixture. She watched the second hand spring forward each second, but it seemed to go in slow motion. She felt her chest tighten up and all of a sudden, the battery powered lantern crashed to the floor.

Chapter 7

"What was that?!" Cora exclaimed. She was just entering the room again when she heard the crash and Milly's loud gasp. Milly opened her mouth to answer, but before any words sounded, out pranced Patty, looking exceptionally proud. Luckily, the lantern was a modern plastic one and hadn't shattered.

"Oh. My. Gosh. That scared me. I thought we were going to be dealing with ghosts, too!" Milly exclaimed. "OK, focus. I'll add the two mixtures together and you stir it 10 times," Milly reminded

Cora. Milly was expecting the mixture to let out a huge smoke cloud or even make some sort of sound, but it was uneventful. Cora placed the cling wrap over the beaker after 10 solid stirs.

"This is going to be the longest overnight EVER. Can I come over right away in the morning so we can test it out?" Milly pleaded.

"Of course! After we try it, we have to go to your house and see if we can understand Angus, though!" Cora exclaimed.

Milly let out a giddy squeal. Was it possible this potion would actually work? The girls decided to call it a day. There would be plenty of time later for reading the rest of the journal and looking at the other recipes.

When Milly and Cora exited the library, Cora's mom just happened to be walking by. Milly's heart stopped. *Is she wondering why we're always in the library?* Milly wondered.

"What are you girls doing? The library isn't for playing. I hope you're not ruining any books," Cora's mom said sternly.

"We're not," Cora quickly answered.

"Could you please bring up this magazine to your uncle? He never misses his Newsweek," Cora's mom said, apparently satisfied that the girls weren't up to anything.

"Sure," Cora obliged.

Milly followed Cora up the stairs and the two stood outside Chester's room. Cora seemed hesitant to knock.

"I-I- I don't want to wake him," Cora explained.

"Does he get mad when he gets woken up or something?" Milly asked.

"No, he's really nice. I just don't know him that well yet," Cora said nervously.

Finally, Cora knocked and gently opened the door. Chester was sitting up in his bed, a pillow against his back. He had a full head of messy white hair and a few sparse whiskers. He had reading glasses hanging on his plaid nightshirt. Patty was sitting right by Chester's side. Chester gave the two girls a shy smile. Milly confirmed to herself that it was the same man she saw last summer.

"Hello Uncle Chester," Cora said, going up to him. "This is my friend, Milly."

"Hi!" Milly said, staying by the foot of the bed.

"Here's your Newsweek," Cora said, handing Chester the magazine.

He smiled, put on his reading glasses, and reached for a pad of paper and pen and he scribbled a message. Milly joined Cora and the two read it together. It read "Nice to meet you Milly. Thanks for the Newseek!" Milly smiled at Chester.

Milly and Cora stood there for a few awkward moments. Chester wrote another message. "Come visit whenever. I get lonely!"

Milly wanted to talk to Chester about the secret room and his flying incident but she wasn't going to be the one to initiate that conversation. Milly thought he seemed like a really nice old man, but she didn't know what he would think of them snooping around his secret room!

***

Angus was bellowing as Milly opened the door, but he wagged his tail and gave her sloppy kisses as soon as he saw who she was. Milly patted his furry head and stared into his eyes. "Angus, you know, I may be able to talk with you tomorrow. Just maybe," Milly whispered. He cocked his head and licked her nose.

"What'd you and Cora do?" Milly's mom said, jolting Milly. Should she tell her mom what they really did? Some of what they did? Milly normally told her mom the truth, but she was pretty sure her mom wouldn't approve of actually drinking the potion made out of mysterious ingredients.

"Oh, the usual. Cora is so fun to hang out with," Milly said, brightening.

"Oh, good!" Milly's mom said enthusiastically.

"Milly still has a friend? Cora hasn't realized how weird you are?" Tommy sneered from the doorway. All Milly could do was ignore him.

***

Milly tossed and turned in her normally cozy bed. She couldn't stop thinking about the next day. *Would the potion work? Would the potion flop? Or worse yet, actually make them sick? If the potion did work, what would that mean exactly? They could understand dogs, sure, but is there much use in that or was it just for fun?* Milly was not only curious and excited, she was also scared. She didn't want to get in trouble with Cora's or her own parents. Milly was a rule follower minus letting Angus go on the couch or little things like that. Was it worth the risk in the name of a fun "mystery solving summer"?

CHAPTER 7 ½

IF HE WAS GOING TO MAKE HIS DEADLINE IN TWO WEEKS, HE WOULD NEED TO BUCKLE DOWN AND GET SERIOUS. PERHAPS TAKE A COUPLE DAYS OFF FROM THE CLINIC. HE COULDN'T BARE LISTENING TO CHILDREN'S LAUGHTER ON HIS DAILY WALK. IT WAS NEAR IMPOSSIBLE TO AVOID PARKS IN ST. PAUL. KIDS. SO MANY KIDS. ALL OUT ON SUMMER BREAK WASTING THE DAY AWAY. KICKING A SOCCER BALL AROUND, SWINGING ON THE PLAYGROUND LIKE SELFISH BABOONS. WHO DO THEY THINK THEY ARE? WHAT PURPOSE ARE THEY SERVING IN SOCIETY? THEY TAKE **AWAY** FROM SOCIETY IF ANYTHING. ABSOLUTELY POINTLESS HUMANS.

AS HE ANGRILY SHUFFLED TEST TUBES AROUND, TRYING TO ORGANIZE HIS WORK STATION, ONE SLIPPED FROM HIS FINGERS AND SHATTERED ON THE CONCRETE FLOOR. HE LET OUT AN ANGUISHED ROAR AS HIS BREATHING GREW FASTER.

He grumbled, "Settle yourself. You will be ready. In two weeks from today, our world will start to improve." He steadied himself against his lab counter until his breathing slowed back down.

Diligently, he swept up the broken glass and repeated the mantra "Kids shall never be kids again."

Chapter 8

Milly woke up late considering the plan for the day. Was she brave enough to drink the potion? After pulling herself out of bed and dressing, she trudged downstairs. There was a pit in her stomach, so the last thing she wanted was a bowl of cereal. She took a banana instead.

"Hey, I'm supposed to take Angus on a walk, but I told Mark I'd go over to his place to play PS4. Can you take him?" Tommy said in a monotone voice.

"Actually, yes," Milly slowly replied and added, "I'm going over to Cora's but we'll come back over here before lunch and take him!" It had to be a sign that she **should** drink the potion and test it out on the walk.

"Calm down, you don't need to write me a book," Tommy said as he left the house.

"You're welcome!" Milly shouted even though he had already slammed the door.

Milly made it over to Cora's and knocked. In less than two seconds, the door swung open. "Hi!" exclaimed Cora. Cora was already holding the lantern, and instead of flashlights, she had a light bulb. The two girls made their way into the library and closed the door. At the antique light fixture, neither girl wanted to be the first to act. Milly wondered whether Cora was also giving herself a pep talk. She must be as nervous as she was.

"Did you tell your parents about the secret room?" asked Cora.

"No," replied Milly.

"Good," Cora stated, relieved.

"Never grow too old or too serious to play," Milly finally said. Without hesitation, Milly scurried in with Cora following. The air was musty and still smelled of vinegar, but sadly no butterscotch anymore. As a Kindergartner, Milly's teacher made all the students taste vinegar on "V" day and it was wretched! Oddly, one boy in the class asked for seconds. Milly's mind jolted back to the present as she watched Cora move a wooden chair so she could reach the light. After screwing in the light bulb she gave the cord a tug and brightness showered over the desk.

"Why didn't we think of this yesterday?" laughed Milly. The potion was sitting on the desk and the vinegar smell became stronger when Milly removed the cling wrap.

"So, who wants to be first?" Cora asked warily.

"I'll do it," Milly said bravely. Like taking off a band-aid, she grabbed the beaker and took one big swig, swallowing before she could think about the taste.

After, she quipped, "Not as bad as it could be I guess. It was like sweet vinegar. Yuck. Sorry, that doesn't sound good at all, does it?" The taste didn't linger, but she let out a loud belch.

Cora laughed as she took her quick swig. Instead of swallowing, she held in the liquid and put her hand over her mouth, her eyes bulging out.

"Just swallow it! You won't taste it as long that way!" Milly exclaimed urgently. Cora nodded silently, and gave an exaggerated swallow.

"OK, that was gross," Cora retorted, "Now how long 'till it works, again?"

Milly fumbled through the loose leafs of paper and came up with the recipe. Her eyes darted back and forth and she said, "One hour. I know, let's kill time by reading the journal again!" Milly spotted it on the desk and turned to the bookmark. They read through some meaningless entries until they came to some interesting updates.

November 2, 1972

We just got back from conferences at Lance's preschool. I have to admit, I am a very proud parent. He can count to over 300 and can *add, he knows all of his letters and is starting to read, and he is very focused on learning. The teachers said he is very academically inclined, though they insist that we encourage him to play with the other kids more. What use is play if he is ahead of all his peers? They will just bring him down. I am tempted to take him out of preschool and just hire tutors. There's only so far that the teachers will push him at preschool. I will discuss this with Betsy, but maybe that's the best route for his future PhD track.*

Milly looked up. Her chest and stomach felt very heavy and constricted upon reading that journal entry. Chester seemed like he was pushing his son Lance way too hard. He was only a preschooler and he didn't let him play at all?

"What's up, Milly?" asked Cora, who had noticed Milly wasn't reading.

"Nothing," Milly responded. Milly didn't want to question Chester and offend Cora. This journal was from 1972 and what's done was done. Was there a point to criticizing Chester's parenting?

Milly looked at her watch and jolted her head up. "It's been almost an hour! Let's go see Angus!"

Chapter 9

When they came up to the front door, Milly and Cora just looked at each other, waiting for the other to make the first move. Finally, Milly cracked open the front door. The loud creaking of the door usually prompted the thunderous barking of a certain dog. They heard no bellowing, no whining, nor barking. Confused, Milly opened the door wider and a proper man's voice yelled, "Who's there? I see you opened my door. You must show your face or at least let me smell you! Who is it? Show yourself!"

"Who's at your house? What the heck…" Cora asked Milly before stopping herself short. Cora just dropped her mouth open and widened her eyes and finally continued, "You don't think…" Angus?" Milly said tentatively as she pushed the door the whole way open.

"Oh, it's you. I should have smelled you a mile away. I missed you so much, you have no idea. I guess when you were gone I was busy and forgot I missed you, but really, now I remember how much I missed you. Milly, Milly, Milly! My favorite person in the world. I love you so much and I love when you bring a friend over! Especially a friend with interesting smells like Cora. She always smells like a cat!" the voice exclaimed rapidly. The words did not line up with Angus's mouth movement at all and his mouth wasn't even open for some of the time. It seemed like it was only in her head.

"Are you hearing everything I'm hearing? He missed me, he loves me, and I'm his favorite person? He loves having you over to smell?" Milly said in disbelief.

"I'm hearing the same. This is so weird! I *have* to be dreaming!" Cora giggled back.

"If you're dreaming then I am too. The potion actually worked, I think!" Milly said in awe. Milly had low expectations that the potion would *actually* work. The girls wandered in the house with Angus smelling the two of them intently.

"I smell the cat again, Milly! You really should bring it over so I can meet it. I promise I won't eat it. Please?" Angus calmly said, as he got over his wild greeting.

"Angus, I'd be more worried Patty would attack you! I know you're such a good dog!" Cora said, rubbing behind his ear.

"Oh, that feels good. More! More!" Angus pleaded as his tail matched his mood, "I don't care if your cat Patty comes over. Sometimes the smell is exciting enough."

"Wait, he can understand us too, I think!" Milly exclaimed. "Angus, would you like to join us for a stroll around the neighborhood?" Milly asked, purposely avoiding the "w" word as Angus always understood that word with or without the potion.

"That sounds lovely! Thank you, I appreciate the offer! When shall we go?" Angus answered. The two girls just laughed and laughed. It was surreal to have a real conversation with a dog. Milly always felt she and Angus had a special bond, but not to this extent.

"I'm not sure I told a joke," Angus started.

"We're not used to talking with dogs. Sorry, Angus!" Cora said.

"Yeah, this *is* weird, what is going on anyway?" Angus asked, as if finally realizing this was out of the ordinary.

"Eh, long story," Milly quickly answered.

Milly grabbed the leash and attached it to Angus's collar and the three of them started out on the walk. It was a beautiful summer day, if a little too hot. They strolled down their street, Howard Ave and took in the happenings of the day: birds chirping, people out and about walking, pebbles waiting to be kicked...

"SQUIRREL! SQUIRREL! Do you see it? Let me get at it! That's my lunch!" Angus interrupted wildly. A middle aged woman who was approaching hunched down and gave the crew a disapproving look. Milly realized the woman was only hearing belligerent, threatening barking from a huge dog.

Milly bent down and whispered in Angus's ear, "Angus, that squirrel isn't for you, and yes I see it. Please be quiet, you're scaring that lady!"

Angus immediately quieted down and remarked, "Oops."

"For real! Angus you are big and to other people you seem scary!" Milly scolded.

"Huh. But I love people! I guess I'll try harder." He had a very distinct embarrassed look on his face. If only they could always communicate this freely! Angus could be the best behaved dog ever!

Walking down the sidewalk, Milly admired Angus's purposeful, leisurely gait. His back was long and elegant, like those regal lion statues that guarded Cora's house.

"Angus, why do dogs like to smell everything? Even really gross stuff?" Cora inquired.

"You know, I don't think the smell of *anything* is gross. Smelling is my way of making sense of things and connections in the world. I never turn down a chance to smell a new person or animal and I never forget a smell," Angus responded thoughtfully.

Their usual route now led them around a corner and Angus found himself nose to nose with a little black and tan Yorkie.

"Dog! Are you a friend or foe?" Angus excitedly demanded. "Let me smell ya', come on!" Angus did the typical dog sniffing as his hair stood straight up on his back. They never met a dog who wasn't intimidated by Angus's size. The little ones usually tried to compensate for being smaller by being mean, but this little dog just looked down.

"I'm cool. Angus, is it? A friend of a friend met you the other day. His name is Frisco. You might remember him. I'm Bella and smell all you want, but I want to smell you too if you don't mind," the Yorkie wavered.

Bella's owner was staring off in the distance, annoyed. He was an older man who didn't acknowledge the dogs or Milly and Cora at all.

"Sure, go ahead. We should play sometime," Angus proposed. He started to bow down with a play invitation. No matter how serious Angus's first impression was, he always turned playful.

"OK, Angus, let's let them walk now," Milly said.

"Yeah, my person isn't much for small talk. Sorry about that!" Bella called over her shoulder as they parted ways.

"See ya' around!" Angus shouted back. Milly and Cora just looked at each other and smirked. The walk was all that they could have hoped for. A dog encounter, a squirrel encounter, and good conversation. Angus now seemed more considerate and wise than Milly ever pictured.

Their walk continued along and Angus entertained the girls with his dog musings. "Ever wonder what's in that guy's garage?" Angus slyly asked. "Besides all his human toys, he keeps his dog's food in an open container that any squirrel, mouse, or dog can just get into! Last week when I ran away, I was like 'Jackpot!'"

"Angus! So that's what you do when you run away?" Milly scolded. She rolled her eyes, but couldn't help but giggle.

"That's awesome," laughed Cora. "At least he's honest!"

They were only a couple houses from Milly's house when a gruff, angry voice shouted, "Get outta' here, you punks! I know what you're up to!" Milly felt the rush of adrenaline shoot to her finger tips and toes.

Chapter 10

Could it be that guy with the fancy sports car?! Milly fearfully looked around to see who was so angry at them. She quickly realized it was the neighbor's dog that always snarled and barked when they passed. She felt relieved, but she did wish that dog would relax.

"Take it easy!!" Cora yelled over. "We aren't 'up to anything'. We are just nice people. And dog." Milly was surprised with Cora's quick defense.

"Your 'nice dog' has pooped in our garden and stolen our newspaper. He's a jerk!" the gruff voice snarled back.

Milly, Cora, and Angus scurried into Milly's house, happy to end that confrontation. "You know, Angus, maybe don't poop in their garden or steal their newspaper, and then maybe he won't hate us so much!" Milly suggested.

"You got it," Angus sheepishly agreed. "But to be fair, I saw him poop on *our* lawn. Dogs, dogs, dogs!"

Milly and Cora almost forgot it was about lunchtime with all that excitement. Milly's mom had already cooked up some chocolate chip pancakes that smelled so good you couldn't ignore it if you tried. As they entered the kitchen to sit at the table, Angus followed and pleaded, "Guys…I want some too! Don't forget about me!" His voice took on a whiney tone that reminded Milly of when he begs at the table.

"Sorry, Angus. Don't you know chocolate can make dogs sick? Besides, you know the rule of not giving you people food!" Milly replied. It was so much harder to turn Angus down when he actually talked to her.

"Really? But I didn't get sick that one time I ate your chocolate Easter bunny! That was way more chocolate!" Angus reminded her. His intent chestnut colored eyes seemed to grab on to her heart strings.

"You could've gotten sick! Chocolate is bad for dogs. End of discussion," Milly scolded, fighting back the urge to just give him a pancake. She sounded like her own mother!

"Am I missing something?" Milly's mom slowly started out. Milly quietly gasped, looking at her mother. She had been so engrossed in her own world she forgot her mom didn't hear Angus's words. She did not want to admit to their magical potion experiments at Cora's house.

"I always talk to Angus! We have a special bond," Milly replied, but Milly's mom was already distracted as she cleaned up after cooking pancakes.

"Mom can't talk to me but you can?" Angus asked.

"Yup, it's a long story," Milly whispered back.

After finishing lunch, the girls excused themselves from the table and ran upstairs to Milly's room. Angus bounded after them. The three of them spent the afternoon sharing stories and laughing together. Angus seemed cooler and cooler the more they got to know him.

***

"Hey turd-sandwich, I asked for the butter," grumbled Tommy. "You know, now that you'll be at the same school as me, PLEASE don't embarrass me. You can't get away with being in la-la-land in 5th grade or people will think you're slow."

"Thanks for the advice," Milly replied sarcastically as she passed the butter. She didn't know how else to talk with her brother anymore.

"Hey, you're welcome," Tommy said, pleased with himself.

"You two, just get along," Milly's dad sighed.

"We are! I gave her advice. She thanked me for it!" insisted Tommy.

"You should really be nicer to me. I took Angus for a walk for you today," Milly reminded her brother. "Would you like a trophy?" Tommy said, rolling his eyes.

After dinner, Milly found herself alone with Angus in her room.

"Why do you let Tommy talk to you like that?" Angus asked Milly.

"He's turned to the dark side. It's too late!" Milly joked dramatically.

"Seriously. Just because he's turning into a teenager doesn't mean you need to lose his friendship," Angus said.

Milly felt a pang in her stomach when she realized how much she missed Tommy's friendship. "Yeah. Angus, you do realize when we wake up in the morning we won't be able to talk with each other anymore? I'm going to miss this!" Milly said, changing the subject.

"You're still my best friend, Milly. It won't change anything," Angus said, licking Milly's face. Angus stayed by her bed until they both drifted off to sleep.

Chapter 11

Even though it was another beautiful, warm Minnesota morning, Milly could only think of the previous day's events. They followed an old recipe using old ingredients and it actually worked! The other recipes probably worked too. Which recipe would they try next? "Feline Translation" was on the top of her list, of course.

What about making "Permanent Mood Enhancement" and slipping it to Tommy? Would he become her friend again? The "permanent" part of it was a little creepy.

Angus was on the couch lazily looking out the window as Milly was about to leave for Cora's house. "Gussy-wus, you know you're not supposed to be on the couch," Milly said half-jokingly. Angus cocked his head and his eyes searched her face for clues, seemingly coming up short. "I already miss talking with you, Angus. Maybe I'll make that potion again sometime," she said hopefully. Angus yawned dramatically and rested his snout on his paws.

Milly stood across the street from Cora's house and took the time to admire the house again, noticing the lion statues, the beautiful porch, the turret, and its overall grandeur. All along, Milly was right in that the house *did* hold a mystery. She must have a better sixth sense than she thought!

"There you are, in la-la land again. Please be… not you," Tommy's voice jolted Milly.

"Cora's house *is* cool. You actually have no idea," Milly replied, refusing to feel rejected. "What are you up to?"

"Meeting Mark at the park to practice soccer," Tommy said. "You don't even know how important my next game is."

As Milly started to cross the street, Tommy stuck his foot out and tripped Milly. She caught herself with her hands and yelled out, "Really?!"

Milly heard Tommy snicker as he jogged away.

As Milly entered Cora's house, they immediately found themselves in the secret room again. Cora opened the journal to where they left off last time.

January 1st, 1973

We pulled Lance out of preschool at the end of term. We hired a nanny who doubles as a tutor and they get along great so far. Lance can keep making strides without peers getting in the way. He is already past Kindergarten level in all subjects. I tried petitioning the private school he will attend next year to allow him to skip Kindergarten (even though he really could skip 1st grade too), but they rejected me. I will keep at it, they haven't even met him yet, so there's no way *they can accurately assess his readiness. I'm sure a little monetary persuasion may help, if you get my gist. All for now!*

"What do you think, Cora?" Milly inquired. She couldn't hold in her thoughts any longer. "Do you think it's the right thing to do to push a little 4 year old that much?

"I don't know. Maybe that's what you gotta do with prodigies?" Cora shrugged.

"Or does it create psychopaths?" Milly immediately regretted her comment, and quickly added, "Or maybe you're right."

"You think my great-great-uncle Chester turned his son, also my relative, into a psychopath? Thanks," Cora said, obviously offended.

"However Lance turned out, Chester had good intentions," Milly offered weakly.

"Yeah, well, I doubt caring enough to give him a good education will make him a bad person."

The two read on in awkward silence. Milly's mind was racing. *Am I totally off base? How can that be a good way to raise a kid? Shouldn't partners in the summer mystery be on the same page? It seemed like in the movies, the best partners came to the same conclusions simultaneously.*

Milly's tummy let out a pleading growl that lasted a good five seconds. The two girls cracked up and Cora said, "Hungry?" Milly felt thankful for the comic relief. The girls wandered to the kitchen where Cora's mom had already started making macaroni and cheese for them.

"Whatcha' girls up to?" Cora's mom said casually.

"Nothing exciting," Cora retorted. Milly wondered whether this was Cora's true feelings on the matter. Milly knew the mystery was not over! Not even because she *wanted* a mystery; she truly had a gut feeling there was more to the story.

After Cora's mom had left the room, Milly whispered, "Let's keep reading after lunch! There will be more clues. I noticed there were more letters attached to the journal!"

"Really? I'm getting kind of sick of sitting there. Especially on such a nice day," Cora replied.

"Oh please, please! I think it's so interesting!"

Cora conceded, and after lunch they skimmed multiple entries until they came to an entry that was interesting.

June 21, 1977

Most kid are at summer camps or wasting away the summer at the pool or getting ticks in the woods. Not my Lance! He is currently being tutored in chemistry, biology, geometry, American history, and Latin. We are trying to concentrate on chemistry, because he seems to take to it. Like his old man, I guess!

Betsy is concerned that he never has any friends over during his free time. I have to admit that when I was a kid I had the best time with my buddies. My favorite was when we went fishing at Green Lake. I offered Lance to have breaks so he can let off a little steam, but he just used that time in the library. I guess he isn't used to free time and wouldn't know what to do with it. I'm not worried, I'm more just really impressed at his focus.

Milly studied Cora's response before saying anything.

"Wow, it's so cool that we have a prodigy in the family! I wonder what he ended up doing in life. I wouldn't be surprised if he won a Nobel Prize," Cora said confidently.

Milly didn't have a response. She thought if she disagreed, Cora might be offended, but she wasn't sure she could fake an agreement.

"I know! Let's make another potion!" Milly suddenly piped up.

Chapter 12

"Wanna try Permanent Mood Enhancement? Evie has been super moody lately. I can't stand to be around her. And you always tell me how awful Tommy is," Cora said.

"Sure!" Milly exclaimed, though she felt a nervous pang in her stomach. Did she really want to give something to Tommy without his knowledge? When she remembered how mean he had been lately, she pushed any doubt out of her mind.

Cora held up the recipe so they could read through it together.

February 1965
Potion for Permanent Mood Enhancement
2 servings
2nd draft

1 1/2 cups liquid iornico
2 tablespoons bosh
2/3 teaspoon dormeck
1 pinch of wanerluv

Dump all ingredients at as close to the same time as possible and wait precisely one minute. Mix with spoon at a very slow, consistent rate for five minutes. Mixture is ready immediately, but can sit for 62 hours before expiring. Results come after one hour and are expected to last a lifetime.

Milly collected the four ingredients while Cora tracked down the measuring cup and spoons. Milly pushed back her instinct of uncertainty that was nagging at her. *Why would you not want to be in a good mood all day, every day? Wouldn't it be a good thing?*

"We could each have two ingredients ready so we could add them all at the same time pretty easily," Cora suggested.

"Right. Yeah, that would work," Milly responded.

Milly opened up the iornico and immediately noticed its thick, fruity smell. It reminded her of that syrup in canned peaches. The other ingredients were blander smelling.

"Ready? 1, 2, 3!" Cora said intently.

They simultaneously released all four ingredients into a glass beaker. Milly had the honors of slowly mixing. Halfway through mixing in silence, Cora finally asked the obviously avoided question. "How are we going to get Evie and Tommy to drink this?"

"Well, the good thing is it smells really good," Milly started.

"Could probably just drink it straight and it'd still taste good," Cora said.

"We could mix them in smoothies!"

"Evie will be totally skeptical of me making her a smoothie, but it may be our only choice," Cora said hopefully.

"I usually put in a banana, frozen strawberries, blueberries, yogurt, and juice. Sound good?" Cora asked as she opened the freezer door. Milly cradled the mason jar with the Permanent Mood Enhancement potion in her arms.

"Yeah, sounds yummy," Milly nodded her head and watched Cora add all the ingredients to the glass blender.

"First let's make some for ourselves, then let's add the potion and make more. Then it won't look so obvious," Cora said confidently.

"Good idea," Milly responded.

After the loud whirring of the blender, Cora quickly poured some of the smoothie out into two cups and Milly emptied the potion into the glass blender. Cora did another quick blend to mix the potion with the smoothie. She poured the "potioned" smoothie into two other cups. Milly wouldn't take her hand off her own smoothie. She did not want to inadvertently take the wrong smoothie!

The loud blender must have roused Evie, as she appeared suddenly in the kitchen. "So... did you happen to make any... extra?" Evie casually asked, much sweeter sounding than she normally was.

"For your information, yes, I was going to offer you some *without* you asking," Cora said with a false irritation in her voice. Cora offered the cup of the "potioned" smoothie.

"Thank you," Evie said dramatically. She took a large mouthful of the smoothie as Milly watched in horror. Milly quickly turned her head because she didn't want to give away anything.

Evie commented, "This is sweeter than I make it but it's really good!"

"Thanks. I like to add some sugar," Cora answered naturally.

"Done!" Cora squealed after Evie was out of earshot. "Let's bring one over to Tommy now!"

Milly's stomach felt full of butterflies. If the potion worked on her brother, maybe she could have his friendship back! She held her smoothie in her left hand and Tommy's in her right hand. Cora skipped by her side holding her own smoothie.

When they entered Milly's house, Angus greeted them enthusiastically, but smelled curiously at Tommy's smoothie while ignoring Milly's. *Angus must smell the potion in it.*

Milly heard the video game blasting from the den. *Won't he be skeptical of this smoothie? I never just give him a smoothie.* Milly thought to herself. A plan quickly developed in her mind, and she led Cora to the noisy den.

"Tommy, settle a debate. Cora and I made smoothies and we want to know which one is better," Milly said confidently.

Cora smirked at Milly, apparently appreciating the idea.

"Which one did *you* make?" Tommy asked, without looking over.

Milly held up the potion-free smoothie, and Tommy immediately replied, "The other one is better."

"No, for real. Just try both and tell me!" Milly pleaded nervously.

Tommy paused his game and motioned for the cups. Milly stared at both smoothies, making sure she remembered which was which. Tommy took a sip out of the regular smoothie. He held it in his mouth, concentrating intently. Then he swallowed and immediately took a sip from the "potioned" smoothie.

Milly held in a gasp and stared at Tommy, waiting for his response.

"Cora's is waaaaay better," Tommy said, handing back the regular smoothie. "In fact, I'll finish it. Thanks. Bye." Tommy resumed the video game and ignored the lingering stares.

It felt too easy. Milly was surprised he actually kept the smoothie and was going to drink it all up. Was she about to get her nice brother back?

***

Milly couldn't wait for dinner so she could see Tommy's results. What if her parents suspected something? There's no way Milly could get away with this, was there?

When Milly's mom announced it was dinner, Milly was the first one at the table. Her foot tapped nervously as she waited for Tommy. It was taking forever! Milly's mom put a steaming bowl of mashed potatoes in the center, then divvied up portions of pork on everyone's plates.

"Could you please give everyone a corn on the cob, Milly?" Milly's mom said sweetly.

"Sure thing," Milly replied. She grasped the tongs and fished out a corn from the big pot on the stove. Suddenly, Milly heard a cheerful version of "I've Got a Lovely Bunch of Coconuts" belted out at full volume.

Milly spun around. Water dripped haphazardly from the corn cob onto the floor. She delivered it to Tommy's plate inconspicuously and smirked to herself as Tommy slid into his seat. His posture was perfectly straight and he playfully held his arm out as he sang, "Thanks Miiiiiilly!" in vibrato.

"Tommy?" Milly's mom said in confusion.

"Yes, mother dear?" Tommy continued singing in an opera-like voice.

"Uhhh, you OK?"

"Never better!" he sang triumphantly. Milly's dad was just entering the kitchen, with an open jaw and wide eyes.

"Tommy you keep us on our toes," Tommy's dad said chuckling.

Milly was very pleased with herself. He was acting weird, but he wasn't mean or mopey! Milly couldn't help but notice Angus staring at Milly. She could swear that he had a disapproving look on his face, but she brushed it off.

Chapter 13

"So....did it work?" Cora's voice said urgently over the phone the following morning.

"Oh my gosh, did it ever. Let's talk about it in person," Milly said excitedly.

When Milly rang the doorbell, Evie opened the door and greeted Milly with a wide smile. "Well hello there, Miss Milly!"

"Hi!" Milly said as Cora pulled her into the library.

"I'll be in my room, but feel free to come visit," Evie called out.

"Weirdo," Cora mumbled as they entered the secret room.

"So it obviously worked on Evie too?"

"Yeah… almost too well. It kinda seems like she's fake or something," Cora said, shrugging her shoulders.

"But better than when she's moody, right?"

"Well, yeah! How's Tommy?"

"Same- he was so funny at dinner last night. He was singing and my parents couldn't stop smiling!"

"Good, I guess!" Cora smirked. "Let's do another potion- this time for us!"

"OK! Let's do Dream Manipulation," Milly suggested. Milly felt like an easy potion, and that seemed like the tamest one.

March 1963
Potion for Dream Manipulation
2 servings
3rd and final draft

Tablet of bogstor
1 teaspoon of feline fur
1 cup hufponce

1 pinch of vivort

Pour the one cup of hufponce into a mason jar or another container that can be tightly sealed and add the pinch of vivort. While you wait for the fizzing to resolve, crush the tablet of bogstor. Crushing the tablet minimizes stirring time for mixture. After the fizzing has stopped, add the crushed tablet. Stir for roughly two minutes. The last ingredient you must add is the feline fur. Let this mixture sit for an hour before shaking vigorously for one minute. (Of course, cover tightly.) Consume, and effects will take place during the next night's sleep.

Cora was already collecting the ingredients when Milly looked up. Almost all of the ingredients were lined up and ready. "Oooh, I don't see the feline fur. Do you think Patty's fur will work?" Cora wondered.

"I don't see why not!" exclaimed Milly. She liked the idea of more actively collecting an ingredient. It made her feel like they had a bigger role in the recipe.

Milly and Cora crept out of the secret room. Milly felt like a spy on a top secret mission. Cora pulled out a pair of hair-cutting shears from the kitchen drawer and they tip-toed down the hallway calling, "Patty!"

"I know where we should probably look first," started Cora.

"Evie's room," Milly and Cora said in perfect unison. Milly smirked and felt content that she was syncing up with her partner in crime. They padded up the stairs and came upon Evie's room. Cora politely rapped on Evie's bedroom door.

"Yeah?" a voice shouted from inside.

"Can we come in?" Cora asked.

"Of course!" Evie belted out, sounding so happy it sounded sarcastic.

They opened the creaky door. Evie had a book open as she was lying on her stomach with her legs in the air, crossed at the ankles. Patty was smugly sprawled, snuggling against Evie's side. Books, clothes, and junk were littered about the floor and her desk. The mess reminded Milly of her own room at her house.

"Yes?" Evie asked sweetly.

"Oh, Milly wanted to see Patty. Can we borrow her for a sec?" Cora implored.

"OK….Good luck!" Evie said charmingly. Patty let out an annoyed meow as Cora scooped her up. They scurried out of the room.

They went back down the stairs and entered Cora's room and plopped themselves on Cora's canopy bed.

"Patty, this will not hurt a bit," Cora calmly murmured. She pulled the sheath off of the scissors and before Cora could snip the fur, Patty bounded out into the hallway. Without hesitation, Milly and Cora followed Patty right up until the cat raced into Chester's room. Milly and Cora stood outside the door, unsure if they should follow the cat.

"What are they trying to do?" Milly and Cora heard a garbled old man's voice say. "Heh. Heh. I think I know what they're doing."

"Did you hear that?" Cora whispered.

"Yeah. Is he talking to Patty?" Milly was immediately taken back to last summer when she saw Chester and the cat deep in conversation.

"Kinda embarrassing… he is losing it a little. Poor guy. C'mon let's try to get Patty back," Cora whispered. She knocked on the half open door and then led them inside.

"Hi Uncle Chester. How are you?" Cora said delicately.

Chester nodded.

"We're trying to play with Patty. Can we take her?" Cora asked tentatively.

"What are you planning to dream about?" Chester softly rasped.

"Oh. Um. I don't know," Cora stammered, surprised.

"Have fun," he garbled, winking. He handed Patty to Cora, who took Patty.

"Thanks!" Milly and Cora said in unison as they made their way back to Cora's room.

"He knows?!" Milly said nervously. *Patty told him!*

"I guess. Seems like he doesn't care," shrugged Cora. Then, quickly and not the least bit dramatically, she snipped off a finger full of fur. Patty was obviously irritated and jumped off the bed immediately following the haircut and bolted back up the stairs towards Evie's room.

"Let's go put together the potion!" Cora exclaimed with wide eyes.

Back in the secret room, Milly and Cora started to put the Dream Manipulation potion together. Cora poured the hufponce in a mason jar and Milly was ready with the pinch of vivort. As soon as Milly let the vivort powder drop in the jar, rapid bubbles formed. Milly and Cora nervously stared while the bubbles reached the top of the jar before slowly receding. They both let out a big sigh of relief. Cora took the tablet of bogstar and began crushing it with a metal spoon. After the bubbles died back down completely, Cora let the pinch of fur fall dreamily into the mixture.

"So… since we have to wait an hour…," started Milly.

"Yes. We can read the journal," Cora interrupted, reading Milly's mind.

May 8th, 1980

I just came back from the awards ceremony at Hilbrook Prep. The principal had let me know beforehand that Lance would be getting an award, but I had no idea that he would be getting department awards in chemistry, calculus, AND Latin. Plus, he got the overall student achievement award for the junior class. He will be graduating next year at only 16 years old. I couldn't stop smiling the whole day. The odd thing is I never once saw Lance smile.

June 30th, 1980

Lance is ready for an introduction to my side hobby. His chemistry base is solid enough now. He is only 15 years old, so the only thing I was worried about is his maturity level. He isn't like other 15 year olds, though, so I decided it is time.

Lance doesn't show much emotion, but for the first time, I swear I could see a smile! He was very interested in all of my developed recipes and he wants to help me. I am so pleased at his response.

October 17th, 1980

When I looked at my secret room again with a new eye, I became suspicious. I usually have a good stockpile of all the ingredients, but when I took inventory, I noticed that I have one less jar of yegim, bogstor, indifre...the list goes on. In short, the ingredients one can use for Canine Obedience, Permanent Mood Enhancement, and Dream Manipulation. I'm trying not to jump to conclusions. I don't believe Lance would take ingredients secretly or without asking. It must be my mistake. I can get lazy and haphazard when I take inventory. Here's a lesson for me, I suppose. Be precise.

Milly looked up from the journal into Cora's eyes and she saw concern. Milly felt it as well. "I need some air," announced Cora.

They found themselves at the kitchen table. Cora absently flipped through the day's mail that was in a pile on the table. All of a sudden Cora muffled her own scream and recoiled from the table, dropping an envelope in front of Milly. The letter was addressed to Chester Endicott.

The return address was from Dr. Lance Endicott.

Chapter 14

"Oh. My. Gosh," Milly stammered. "Is this from today? Is this real?" Milly pointed to the date that was stamped on the letter, and it said August 21st 2019.

"Uh, I guess! It can't be the same Lance, can it?" Cora stammered.

"I wonder if your mom knows about that letter. Can we go open and read it in your room?" Milly asked. She stared at the name Dr. Lance Endicott and got a shiver up her spine. Seeing the whole name put together really gave her a sense she *had* seen that name in another context.

"Evie must've brought in the mail since my mom's still out," reasoned Cora. "I've seen my mom open his mail before. This isn't any different! Let's do it!"

The girls scurried upstairs to Cora's room and gingerly closed the door. Seated on Cora's bay window seat, Cora opened the envelope as carefully as possible, like it was the Declaration of Independence in her hands. The letter was handwritten in neat penmanship.

August 20th, 2019

Dear Dad,

I know you prefer old-fashioned hand-written notes. How is your health?

The reason I am writing is I am humbly asking for your guidance. Let's say I put together a revolutionary medicine for children in particular. I was thinking there are two strong possibilities on how to distribute it, one being through the water source in the schools and the other being a vaccination program carried out in the schools. As a medical doctor I can make the vaccinations appear unquestionably legitimate. I know with both options we won't be able to get every single child dosed, but which way would get the biggest percentage? Or do you believe drinking is more or less effective than a shot? Obviously there are different factors I'm considering. I do not want to screw up.

Like a good scientist, before mass administration I plan to test my formula on two children from my clinic- one boy and one girl, probably by way of vaccination. This will be done within the week.

I must figure this out. I would love to begin the process right away at the beginning of the school year. Think of how those teachers will love me. Please write back as I clearly have a deadline- about a week from now is when school starts. Thank you in advance!

    Sincerely,

      Your son, Dr. Lance Endicott

"I-I-I don't even know what to say," Cora spluttered. Milly sat there silently trying to fully grasp what she had just read. The letter was very vague but she had a gut feeling that whatever Lance was up to was no good, even if the teachers were going to love him.

"This is so creepy. Is there a way we can ask Chester for help on this?" Milly asked. "I don't think Chester would approve of giving kids a medicine without them knowing."

"I agree. I guess we can try to talk to Chester," Cora said thoughtfully.

They crept over to Chester's room. The door was ajar already, so after a delicate rap on the door, they tiptoed in. Chester was awake and eyed them in surprise.

"Uncle Chester, your son Lance wrote a letter to you," Cora started, wasting no time. "It sounds like he is planning to give kids in schools a 'medicine' either through the water supply or vaccines. He wants your help, but I don't think whatever he is planning is good."

Chester's eyes went wide. He motioned for the notepad and pen on the nightstand by his bed. After receiving it, he jotted a message down in shaky handwriting. "Stop him. Don't tell your parents about it." His hands were still shaking after writing the message, and he let the pen fall carelessly on his bed.

Cora consented, "OK, we won't tell my parents."

Chester grasped the pen again and wrote "Thank you. He is dangerous." His breathing was getting faster and wheezier.

"I think we need to let him rest now," Cora said softly.

Milly searched Chester's eyes before saying, "We got this, Chester. You rest." She was surprised at her own confidence just now, but she knew she and Cora were meant to stop Lance.

The girls made their way back to Cora's room and Milly let herself get lost in thought. *Whatever Lance had planned, it seemed like it was only directed at children and somehow there would be a benefit to teachers. Lance wants as many children to get the "medicine" as possible. Is there a relationship between Chester's potions and Lance's "medicine"? Could he be using Chester's old recipes and tweaking them to use for another purpose? The scariest question of all: what would that use be?* Milly remembered that Chester talked of missing ingredients to a few different potions, which gave her a shiver up her spine.

Cora's voice interrupted Milly's thought process. "OK, we need to act fast. What should we do? Tell our parents? I know Chester said not to, but why would he want us to go at this alone?"

Milly felt a tiny surge of disappointment. There's no doubt the best thing to do would be to tell their parents. Was the mystery bigger than them when it was concerning the lives of children, including potentially both of their own lives?

"I agree, I think we do need to tell our parents. Let's each tell our own parents tonight," Milly conceded. She wanted to try the "Dream Manipulation" potion before they told their parents. One last hurrah. Cora tucked the letter under her pillow before they made their way back to the secret room.

Milly noticed the dream manipulation potion was now a deep purple, whereas before it had been as clear as water. She tightened the lid with all her might so she could finish the last step of shaking the jar. When she opened the jar, Cora announced, "I'll go first this time!"

The two girls each took turns gulping their portion of the potion. It seemed like no big deal this time. All Milly could think of was that it was probably the last time she would be drinking a potion in the secret room if they were going to tell their parents everything.

***

Milly sat motionless at the dinner table as her mom placed a chicken drumstick on her plate. "What's wrong, honey?" Milly's mom asked.

Milly froze as she was put on the spot. She was still debating with herself on what to say. Her parents were never going to believe her and what if they don't even let her go over to Cora's house anymore? No, she decided she would not say a word about this to her parents.

"Does it have anything to do with that code you asked me to break?" Tommy said innocently. His eyes bored into her own. Even with that intense eye contact, his eyes appeared weirdly vacant.

"No! That was just for fun. It's just that I have a bit of a headache," Milly quickly lied.

"You're probably dehydrated. Drink more water," her dad offered. That was always his go-to solution no matter what Milly complained about.

Milly exhaled deeply but softly. Thankfully no one had taken Tommy's comment seriously. Milly felt relieved, but wondered how the conversation was going at Cora's house. What if *her* parents would put a halt to their summer mystery?

After dinner, Milly dialed up Cora's house's phone in her room. Cora answered on the first ring, "Hey. What'd your parents say?"

"Hey. I chickened out and didn't tell them," Milly admitted.

"What?! No way. I didn't tell my parents either. I just don't think they are ready for this kind of drama. What are we going to do now?" Cora replied.

"Let's sleep on it," suggested Milly.

"Don't forget- we can control our dreams tonight- if it works, I mean," Cora reminded Milly.

"Ha! Yes! What are you going to dream about?" Milly asked.

"I want to fly around the world and see all kinds of animals," Cora said dreamily. "What about you?"

"I'm going to crack the case," Milly said plainly.

CHAPTER 14 ½

HE SMILED CONTENTEDLY IN HIS BED AS THE MOON SHONE THROUGH HIS WINDOW. HE COULDN'T REMEMBER THE LAST TIME HE WAS THIS HAPPY. PERHAPS WHEN HE FIRST CAME UP WITH THE PLAN? HE WAS OFFICIALLY READY FOR THE NEXT STAGE IN OPERATION OBEDIENCE OF CHILDREN.

HE WOULD NEED ONE BOY AND ONE GIRL AS HIS TEST SUBJECTS. FOR THE BOY, HE HAD HIS EYES SET ON A KID WHO WAS NOT ONLY HIS PATIENT AT HIS CLINIC, BUT HE ALSO SAW HIM FREQUENT THE PARK NEAR HIS HOUSE. HE OVERHEARD HIM TALKING WITH HIS FRIEND ABOUT VIDEO GAMES; WHICH LEVEL IN A GAME THAT HAD SECRET DOORS AND WHICH GAMES HE WANTED TO BUY NEXT. WHAT MONEY ARE YOU BUYING THESE GAMES WITH, KID? HIS DAD WORKED TIRELESSLY AT HIS WORTHWHILE JOB AND HIS MOM PUT MEALS ON THE TABLE AND WAS BASICALLY HIS SERVANT- WHAT- SO HE COULD PLAY HIS LITTLE VIDEO GAMES? WHAT A WORTHLESS EXISTENCE. THE BOY WAS A LITTLE OLDER THAN HE

ORIGINALLY HAD PLANNED FOR HIS FIRST EXPERIMENT, BUT HIS BEHAVIOR WAS SO TROUBLESOME, HE ACTUALLY FELT SORRY FOR THE KID.

THE GIRL HE DECIDED ON WAS A NEW PATIENT IN HIS SCHEDULE THAT WAS COMING THE SAME DAY AS THE BOY. HE KNEW LITTLE ABOUT HER, BUT HE PURPOSELY WANTED ONE OF THE SUBJECTS TO BE RANDOM.

HIS PLOT WAS BRILLIANT. IT WOULD BE DOCTOR'S ORDERS THAT THE TEST SUBJECTS WOULD NEED A "VACCINATION" AND HE WOULD THEN SCHEDULE A FOLLOW-UP FOR SOME MADE-UP CONCERN FOR THE FOLLOWING WEEK. HE WOULD BE ABLE TO STUDY THE RESULTS AND EITHER TWEAK THE RECIPE OR, HOPEFULLY, HIS POTION WOULD PROVE TO BE READY FOR MASS ADMINISTRATION. HE COULDN'T HELP BUT ADMIRE HIS OWN MARVELOUS MIND.

IF THE POTION WAS SUCCESSFUL, HE REALLY ONLY HAD ONE MORE STAGE OF THE OPERATION, AND HE WAS WAITING ON SOME ADVICE ON THE LOGISTICS. THE WORLD WOULD NEVER BE ABLE TO REPAY HIM, BUT HE BELIEVED IT WAS HIS PURPOSE IN THE WORLD. WHAT A SELFLESS MAN, HE THOUGHT PROUDLY OF HIMSELF.

Chapter 15

Milly was at the police station. Policemen and women were wandering around, in and out of offices and cubicles. They looked busy but when Milly took a closer look, they were aimless with vacant looks on their faces.

Milly took one policeman aside and urgently whispered, "I have to tell you something!"

"I don't deal with children," the policeman replied stoically and scurried away.

Milly saw Cora waiting for her at the exit of the police station. The two girls left and walked straight to the school, which was two blocks away. Every adult they passed on the sidewalk kept their chin up high and avoided any eye contact. Nevertheless, Milly felt determined and empowered.

Milly and Cora arrived at the school building after what seemed like only seconds. Milly stopped in her tracks to observe the scene. Little kids ranging from Kindergarten to 4th grade were streaming in the school building. Lots of giggles and cheerful banter filled the air. Milly spotted a tall man in a white doctor's coat and a tan cowboy hat standing by the entrance. His face was somewhat generic and he had dark brown hair and a goatee. He held a brown leather briefcase. Milly stopped in her tracks and stared squarely at him until his eyes met hers.

Milly marched up to him and urgently yelled, "Hey! Are you Lance?"

The man did not drop their eye contact and replied thinly, "I prefer *Dr*. Endicott. Who are you?"

"What is in your briefcase? Is it the 'medicine'?" Milly asked using her fingers as air quotes. She put her hands on her hips and made herself as imposing as possible. Cora stood silently, but comfortingly by her side.

"For your information, yes, it is," Lance shrugged.

Milly could see the embroidery on the white coat more clearly and above Lance's name was "Health-Garden Clinic", the name of the pediatric clinic she goes to for check-ups and when she's sick. It finally hit her- this was *her* doctor! Her family mostly calls their pediatrician "Dr. E", but she knew the name had sounded familiar. Despite this big realization, Milly stuck to business, "I know Chester Endicott. He said the 'medicine' won't work."

"I don't believe you. If you know so much, what is the 'medicine' supposed to do?" Lance countered.

"Uh. It's going to make children… very smart… and always happy…?" Milly guessed with less confidence than she was going for.

"I don't think you know Chester and you don't know anything about my medicine. Nice try," Lance said dryly.

Without a second thought, Milly charged toward the man and grabbed the briefcase. Before she turned to run away, Milly flicked Lance's nose as hard as she could and stuck her tongue out at him

Milly and Cora giggled as they fled the school grounds. In no time they were sitting in Milly's kitchen with the briefcase. The briefcase was locked but Milly slyly pulled out a key from her jean shorts pocket. Inside, they found hundreds of syringes filled with clear liquid, plus a recipe card tucked in a side pocket. The recipe card was too blurry to read; Milly couldn't even make out the title.

Milly and Cora found themselves at a medical waste dump site. She didn't even wonder how they got there as that didn't matter. Milly and Cora held armfuls of syringes on a platform overlooking a huge pile of trash spanning at least half a mile across. Milly yelled "OK!" and the two girls leaned over the railing and emptied the loads. The crime-stoppers gleefully high-fived each other. "Mission accomplished!" Milly announced.

Chapter 16

Milly lied on her bed, smiling. She finally opened her eyes and jolted her head up. That dream was surreal! The "Dream Manipulator" worked... to a point. If she could totally have her way, she would have found out what potion recipe Lance was going to use, and be able to stop him using her mental ingenuity, not by simply swiping the briefcase. In real life, she knew that she couldn't rely on her speed or anything physical against a grown man. He would be on high alert. A good idea suddenly popped in her head. Before Milly even ate breakfast, she dialed Cora up.

"Hello?" a voice answered.

"Cora!" Milly blurted out before realizing it was Evie who had answered the phone. "I mean, is Cora there, please?"

Milly heard Evie snicker before lazily replying, "Yeah, one sec. Silly Milly!"

"Hey," started Cora.

"Cora, do you still have the envelope from Lance's letter?" Milly inquired, wasting no time.

"Umm..." Cora wavered. Milly could tell Cora was running up the stairs. "Yeah, it's still on my desk in my room. Why?"

"Can I come over?" Milly wondered.

"Give me 15 minutes. I need to eat and get dressed. You're up early, sheesh!"

"K. Bye!" Milly was so excited she nearly forgot she needed to dress and eat too.

***

"Wait till we get in my room," Cora whispered as soon as she opened the front door. Milly politely greeted Evie and Cora's mom before heading upstairs. When Cora closed the door behind them, Cora said, "OK. What's up?"

"The police will never believe us. We have to take care of this ourselves," Milly began.

"You know, this is serious business. Just because neither of us told our parents, doesn't mean we don't need to involve grown-ups," Cora said.

"In my dream last night, I tried to get the police to help us and they wouldn't bother with me. I think that dream was telling me certain things," Milly explained.

"Hmm, do you have a better idea then?" Cora asked skeptically.

"Let's write back, pretending to be Chester. We can fish more information out of him!" Milly exclaimed. "We'll type it out- he won't be able to tell from our handwriting. We'll make up some advice, find out exactly when and where he'll carry out the plan, and stop him. The return address is on the envelope so we know how to get the letter to him."

Cora sat there motionless. Her face didn't give away her inner thoughts. "Well, that could work, maybe," Cora replied. All Milly could do was squeal with joy.

"By the way, how was your dream?" Milly said, forcing herself to slow down.

"So awesome! I flew around all night exploring the world! It wasn't scary, but it was so exhilarating! I remembered that I could control my dreams, so I got to see all my favorite animals: monkeys, lions, elephants, everything! I even went to see polar bears- and somehow I wasn't even cold! What was your dream like?"

"I cracked the case, but only because in my dream I was faster than him. It was kind of disappointing because I never found out what the potion was for and I didn't get Lance to listen to me. I did steal the potion, though. You were there, and we threw all the syringes into a medical waste dump," Milly said. She wasn't sure she wanted to disclose that Lance might be her doctor quite yet.

"Whoa, your dream was a little, um, different than mine," giggled Cora.

"Can we use your computer to write the letter?" Milly asked abruptly.

"I guess you're ready to start, huh?" Cora said as she pulled out the chair and motioned Milly to sit at the desk.

"It's fresh on my mind," Milly reasoned. Milly pulled up the word app and immediately began typing.

August 23rd, 2019

Dear Lance,

My health is good, thank you for asking.

Did you end up using my recipe for "Permanent Mood Enhancement" as the main base? I am curious what you have named the new potion and its exact purpose. Which schools are in your plan?

As far as vaccinations versus water supply, I would go with vaccinations. You may end up needing to do more leg work beforehand, but you will have more control of the doses this way. Kids these days would rather have a can of soda pop than a glass of water. At least with a vaccination it's in their bodies with one prick.

Answer promptly, as I can help with more issues you may encounter.

All the best,

    Your father

Cora looked stunned as she read the letter. "You sound just like an old man! 'Kids these days!'" laughed Cora. "But, why did you encourage vaccinations?" Cora shuddered.

"I learned a lot from all of those journals!" Milly answered. "And I think if he just put it in the water supply he'd be over and done with it a lot quicker. With vaccinations, he'll have a lot more to do which gives us more time to stop him. Plus it seems like it'd be more effective, so Lance would have to agree," she added.

"Yeah that makes sense," agreed Cora. "Now let's print this off and address this sucker so we can get it in the mail today!"

Milly was taken aback Cora's sudden motivation and she liked it. "Agreed!"

Cora grasped the empty envelope. Milly wrote out the address with penmanship as close to her Chester's handwriting as she could; kind of messy, but experienced.

After placing the letter carefully in the mailbox, Cora shrugged and said, "Now what?"

Milly sighed and murmured, "Wait?" The adrenaline that had been coursing through Milly's body was now completely gone. Part of their plan included lots of patience.

Chapter 17

After lunch at Cora's, the girls needed to take a break from the journal, so they decided to go to Milly's house and take Angus for a walk. The day was clear with not one single cloud in sky.

Milly shouted, "Hello?" With no response, they wandered in the kitchen. On the counter Milly noticed a note. This was a common way to communicate in her family.

"Milly- took Tommy to his check-up at Health-Garden, but call the police if we're not home by 1. - Mom". Under the writing, a humorous smiley face signified she wasn't serious about the police thing. Tommy was at his doctor right now. Her doctor. Lance Endicott? Milly felt a wave of nausea and couldn't speak. Was Lance giving Tommy the "vaccination"? Little did her mom know that maybe calling the police *wasn't* such a bad idea.

Their walk with Angus was quiet. Milly was deep in thought over Tommy. *What if he's getting the potion right now?! Should I tell Cora that I think Lance is my doctor?* She suddenly felt a wave of guilt flood through her. She regretted giving Tommy the Permanent Mood Enhancement. She felt no better than Lance, who was trying to change children's personalities. *Shouldn't people just be who they're supposed to be? Does Cora regret giving Evie the potion? How do I feel about Cora if she doesn't regret it!?*

Milly's mind sprung back to the present when they arrived back at Milly's house and she saw her mom and brother standing in the kitchen.

"Oh hi, girls!" Milly's mom exclaimed brightly. "You saw my note, Milly?"

"I did. I almost called the police," Milly laughed uneasily.

"Yeah, sorry. I thought we'd be home earlier. Traffic was horrendous with all that construction," she sighed in exasperation.

Milly studied Tommy's face. *Did Lance Endicott give him the evil potion in a vaccine at the clinic? Was Tommy one of the 'test subjects' Lance had written about?*

"Cora, let's watch YouTube videos up in my room," Milly said, giving Cora a look to mean she actually had other plans. It was time to tell Cora that Tommy's doctor, her doctor, was probably Lance Endicott, the same one they were on a mission to stop.

"Actually, I have to get home. I have a doctor check-up soon. I forgot to tell you," Cora said nonchalantly. Before Milly could protest, Cora was out the door. In horror, Milly watched her run across the street.

When Milly went to look back at Tommy, he was already gone, probably in his room. Which Tommy was it? The newly happy Tommy or the zombie

Tommy? She sadly realized she wanted the old, moody Tommy back.

***

Milly's mom called everyone to the dinner table around 6. She urgently insisted that they all eat their spaghetti and meatballs quickly, because otherwise Tommy might be late for his important soccer game.

"Oh, I forgot to tell you. I already called the coach to let him know that I quit. No need to rush through dinner, everyone," he announced calmly.

Milly dropped her fork, making a loud clanging against her plate and just stared at her parents, waiting for their responses.

"What do you mean, Tommy? Is this a joke?" Milly's dad said, half-smiling.

"I don't joke. It's no secret I'm not the team's best player, and honestly, even the best players on the team will not be even close to becoming professional players. It's a waste of time if you don't have a real shot at the big leagues," Tommy stated seriously.

"Tommy, you're so good at soccer! Yes of course we know it's not likely any players on your team will actually become professional, but you have so much fun playing! Plus I thought tonight's game was important!" Milly's mom said enthusiastically.

"Even if I eventually made the varsity team in high school, the percentage of high school players that end up playing in the pros is 0.04%. I was not blessed with the right genetics to make it big. No offense. I know that I was blessed with a decent brain, so I decided to just concentrate on school. Sure, I guess that game is important to some kids, but it's **just a game**," Tommy remarked in a monotone voice.

"What has gotten into you?" Milly's dad asked.

Milly knew.

CHAPTER 17 ½

LANCE, STILL AT THE NOW EMPTY CLINIC AND FINALLY FINISHED WITH HIS DAY-JOB CHARTING, JOTTED DOWN HIS NOTES FROM HIS FIRST TWO EXPERIMENTAL PATIENTS. "MALE, 13 YRS. PRE-VACCINATION: SUBJECT WAS CHEERFUL, BUT WHEN ASKED OF HIS HOBBIES, SUBJECT LISTED SOCCER, VIDEO GAMES, TV, AND PLAYING WITH OTHER KIDS IN THE NEIGHBORHOOD. WHEN ASKED WHAT HE WANTED TO DO WHEN HE WAS OLDER, SUBJECT ANSWERED, 'PROFESSIONAL SOCCER PLAYER'. SUBJECT HAS BEEN OBSERVED AT THE SOCCER FIELD IN THE PAST AND SHOWS NO EXTRAORDINARY TALENT, LEADING TO THE CONCLUSION THAT SUBJECT DEMONSTRATES SKEWED SELF-AWARENESS AND OVERESTIMATION OF SKILLS. WHEN ASKED ABOUT HIS FAVORITE AREA IN SCHOOL, SUBJECT ANSWERED, 'RECESS'. DELIVERED

2 CCS OF 'M1W2 FLU VACCINATION', AKA 'OBEDI-
ENCE OF CHILDREN' POTION AT THE END OF THE
VISIT. TOLD MOTHER OF SUBJECT THERE WAS CON-
CERN OF A BUG BITE ON HIS BACK AND ARRANGED
FOR FOLLOW-UP IN ONE WEEK. APPOINTMENT SET-
TLED ON NEXT TUESDAY MORNING."

HE SMILED TO HIMSELF, AND CONTINUED WRIT-
ING NOTES. "FEMALE, 10 YRS. PRE-VACCINATION:
SUBJECT WAS UNUSUALLY CHATTY, TALKING ABOUT
HER LAST DREAM, WHAT HER FAVORITE MOVIES ARE;
GENERALLY VERY USELESS CONVERSATION. WHEN
ASKED ABOUT HER FAVORITE SUBJECT IN SCHOOL,
SHE REPLIED, 'LUNCH AND RECESS'. CANDIDATE
WAS MORE THAN SUITABLE TO TEST MEDICINE. DE-
LIVERED 2 CCS OF 'M1W2 FLU VACCINATION' AKA,
THE 'OBEDIENCE OF CHILDREN' POTION AND ONCE
AGAIN WE SCHEDULED A FOLLOW-UP IN ONE WEEK
CONCERNING A BUG BITE."

HE HAD NO DOUBTS THAT THE MEDICINE WOULD
HAVE THE DESIRED RESULTS. ONCE HE CONFIRMED
THIS, HE COULD START MASS ADMINISTRATION, BUT
OF COURSE HE HAD TO DECIDE BETWEEN VACCINA-
TIONS AND WATER SUPPLY.

HE CURSED HIMSELF FOR HIS LACK OF SELF-
CONFIDENCE IN CARRYING OUT THE PLAN ALL ON
HIS OWN. HE KNEW HE WAS SMART ENOUGH, YET
WHY DID HE NEED HIS FATHER'S ADVICE?

HIS GOOD MOOD TURNED SOUR, AND HE TRIED TO
PUMP HIS SELF-ESTEEM BACK UP. HE STARED AT HIS
DIPLOMAS ABOVE HIS DESK. HIS PLAN TO MASTER A

POTION STARTED IN MEDICAL SCHOOL, WHICH DROVE HIM TO GO INTO THE FIELD HE DESPISED THE MOST-PEDIATRICS. OF COURSE, MOST DOCTORS CHOSE PEDIATRICS BECAUSE THEY LOVE KIDS, BUT NOT LANCE. THERE WAS NOTHING WORSE THAN FACING KIDS EVERY DAY, BUT THIS IS WHAT ONE CALLS DISCIPLINE; PUSHING THROUGH THE AWFUL WITH COMPLETE FOCUS ON THE END GOAL. THE WORLD WOULD BE FOREVER IN HIS DEBT.

Chapter 18

Milly hadn't heard from Cora in a couple of days and she was starting to wonder why. She wanted to give Cora space, although she desperately wanted to share the new developments. Tommy was so obviously different, even from the "Mood-Enhanced" Tommy that she'd be surprised if he *hadn't* gotten the vaccination. She had overheard her parents talking in their bedroom the other morning. They were wondering if Tommy was already past the attitude phase and into the adult phase. He was too young, they had decided. They didn't seem that concerned, though.

That was because they had no idea what really happened at the doctor.

Milly rubbed behind Angus's ears while he groaned contentedly. The more she thought about how Lance gave him the evil potion, the more guilty she felt that she gave him something too. Here she was, understanding he got something awful and probably permanent at the evil doctor's visit, yet she did the same thing, albeit she was trying to give him something that made him a happier person. She knew in the back of her mind it didn't matter what the potion was for- it was an unnatural, irreversible change.

"Angus, you knew the smoothie we gave to Tommy was bad news, didn't you? It was only Permanent Mood Enhancement- much better than whatever he got at the doctor," she said trying to defend herself. She was so sad that she may have lost Angus's respect.

The phone jolted her upright. She ran to answer, desperately hoping it was Cora.

"Hello?" Milly said cautiously.

"Hey," Cora answered plainly. Her voice showed no emotion either way."Can you come over?"

"I'll be right there," Milly replied.

Tommy appeared in the living room. His face seemed vacant and creepy. She eyed him nervously, waiting for him to speak. When he didn't, she finally said, "I'm going to Cora's. Could you tell mom?"

"I will do that for you. When shall I tell her you will be back?" he said in an robotic voice.

"I don't know, I'll call her if I stay for lunch," she said slowly, studying his face.

"OK, Milly. I will just be in my room previewing my text books for the school year."

Milly shuddered and bounded out the door. He wasn't acting evil… he wasn't acting rude or anything "bad" in particular. He was just acting like he had no brain, no personality.

***

Just like her voice on the phone, Cora's face didn't show any hint of emotion when she opened the front door for Milly. The windows were finally open in Cora's room, as the days weren't quite as hot anymore and they didn't have the air conditioner running. It was a jarring reminder that school would be starting soon.

Sprawled out on Cora's desk were five different text books. "Oh, whose are these?" Milly said, surprised.

"I asked my mother if we could pick up my text books early at school," Cora said.

"Uh, why?" Milly said, laughing. She thought Cora was joking until Cora's face showed no sign of humor.

"What else would I do with my last week before school starts?" Cora said, almost defensively. "I invited you over because I thought you might want to look over the textbooks with me."

"Or... we could read that journal?" Milly asked meekly. She was starting to get confused. She realized she hadn't known Cora during the school year yet. *Maybe she is a really serious student.*

"Oh, this? This is a waste of time. Do you realize we're only children? This is absolutely none of our business. What we need to concentrate on is age-appropriate learning," Cora said, firmly grasping the journal.

Milly eyed the journal nervously, when suddenly a realization came to her like getting splashed with cold water. *She got Lance's "vaccine".*

"Did- did- did you get a... vaccine... yesterday?" Milly asked carefully.

"A flu vaccination. Did you know that the flu costs the economy 10.4 billion dollars every year?" Cora said in a monotone voice.

"Yeah, I get flu shots every year too, but I do NOT think you got the flu shot yesterday," Milly sputtered.

"Fewer than 60% of American children got the flu shot last season," Cora went on, "Dr. E wants it to be 100%."

Milly gasped. "Cora! Dr. E! My brother got the shot too. Both of you got the evil medicine that Lance wants to give to all children!"

"The economy will benefit from healthy individuals. Anyways, what do you think we should start with first? I'll let you decide because I'm eager for all of the subjects."

"We don't even have to read the journal, I don't care! Let's just go to the playground! Or we could play Legos? I have a new set- totally unopened!" Milly desperately shrieked.

"I'm not a total natural at math, so I suppose that's all the more reason we should start with that," Cora said, ignoring her. She started thumbing through the different sections. "Ooh! Dividing by fractions. I always had a hard time with this. How about you? If neither of us gets it, I suppose we could ask Evie for help."

Milly knew it was hopeless. At this point, she had to think of what to do next. She noticed the journal was on the desk. While Cora was feverishly scanning the explanation page of dividing fractions, Milly slowly pulled the journal off the desk and discreetly tucked it in her waistband on her back.

A cheerful voice from downstairs announced, "Lunch is on the table!" Cora's mom had made some sandwiches and fruit bowls. A stack of letters was untouched on the table. Cora's mom had her back to the table, busily unloading the dishwasher, putting clean dishes away. Cora had brought the math book down and was still studying the book intently. Milly, keeping a watchful eye on Cora and her mom, flipped through the letters until she came to a letter addressed to Chester with Lance as the return sender again! Milly tucked it safely with the journal.

"Actually, I don't think I can stay for lunch," Milly said carefully.

"Too bad!" Cora's mom exclaimed, her hand on her hip and a disappointed expression on her face. Cora didn't even look up from the math book when Milly got up and left the kitchen.

As Milly jogged across the street, she felt so confused and helpless. Her new best friend was totally changed. She had to figure out how to get her back to normal! As soon as she got to her room, Milly made sure the door was closed, then collapsed on the bed on her stomach. She urgently opened the letter.

July 7th, 2018

Dear Father,

Thank you dearly for your prompt reply. I would come talk to you in person, but it seems the relatives you live with now are always there. I have no desire to meet them.

I didn't know you were interested in my project! I would have included you more throughout the process, but you had said before that I should stay away from potion-making! What changed your mind?

This must remain top-secret. Do not tell anyone the contents of this letter. I'm not even comfortable putting this on paper, but I do trust you. Please just destroy the letter when you are through reading it.

As you should already know, all my life I have detested my peers. At school, they did nothing but hinder my learning. They were immature, unmotivated, and well, would rather play outside, play sports, what-have-you, instead of devoting all of their time to their school work. I never had one single friend my age. My friends were you, mother, and my teachers. And I liked it that way. The teachers all loved me because I never disrupted class and I turned in all my homework on time. I know they must have been so frustrated with the others.

I'm letting myself go on a tangent, I apologize. I am just giving you a background in why I developed the new recipe. You are correct in that I did use the Permanent Mood Enhancement, but it wasn't my base. I only really needed the element of "permanence". I also tied in Dream Manipulation and Canine Obedience. I had to come up with all new concoctions, though, to finalize the potion. Against my true wishes (which would have been "Mindless Angels Transformation") I named the recipe "Obedience of Children". That title is basically a euphemism and not totally inclusive of what it will do. Not only am I turning as many kids as I can to be blindly obedient and absent of any child-like personality, but it will make them driven to learn. They will have no interests in anything non-academic. I will make the classroom a dream for teachers and I am certain in the long run we will have smarter and more serious college students (and beyond).

The downside of my plot is that I believe it doesn't sound that favorable to the public. They wouldn't see the big picture, which is why I have to take matters into my own hands and wait for them to thank me later.

I think you're right in that a vaccination course would be the most effective. Yes, more work, as you pointed out, but it's worth it. I will be making phone calls to the school districts on behalf of a Public Health Advocate employee from the Department of Public Health. I have a special app on my cell phone that allows my number to be disguised as a reputable number from the Department of Public Health. Fool-proof. I will notify them that there is a new, deadly flu virus suddenly taking over parts of the country, and that children will be receiving the new vaccine first as they are the most at risk. When schools get orders from the Department of Health they will be inclined to listen. Then I, personally, will administer the "vaccine" to each and every child in the city. When I hit the full-scale production of the potion, I can eventually recruit trustworthy employees to administer the vaccine across the state, and then the country. It may take a long time, but I do agree with you that this will be the most effective route.

St. Paul schools start right after Labor Day. I already devised a schedule for each school in my planner. I want to waste no time.

I'm set in my plan, but as always I welcome your input. Anything I'm missing? Or something I should do differently? I trust my father.

> *Sincerely,*
>
> *Your son, Dr. Lance Endicott*

Milly shot off the bed and backed away from the letter as if the letter itself was soaked in the potion. Milly felt a shiver go all the way up her spine and her arms were covered in prickly goose bumps. Her heart felt loud in her chest. Milly felt the burning sensation of tears building in her eyes.

I'm in this alone now. I can't even brainstorm with Cora anymore. What am I going to do!? She knew that she had to find out when he would be giving the shots at her school. She could NOT let herself get into a situation where she could get the shot. Once she knew the schedule, then she could concentrate on the antidote. How could she find out the schedule? All of a sudden, she murmured out loud, "Angus can help."

Chapter 19

Milly had a plan. She would give herself another round of the Canine Translation, then she would explain to Angus how he could help. She would put a GoPro camera on his head and he would run to Lance's house. Somehow he would get in, then he would do spy work there. He would find the schedule book or calendar that says when and where the vaccines would be given. It was a little ambitious, but it could work.

How could she get back in that secret room? Or even back in her house? She could fake some school-related interest, then at some point she could sneak into the secret room and put the potion together.

Milly nervously dialed her friend's number.

"Hello, this is Cora," came out from the phone receiver.

"Hi Cora, this is Milly. I was wondering if you wanted to look over our new science book."

"I'm in the middle of going over math with my mom, but how about in a couple hours?" Cora said. She didn't even sound surprised.

"Sounds good, thanks Cora!" Milly replied in faux-excitement. She hung up the phone and let out a big breath.

***

"Good afternoon!" chirped Evie as she opened the front door. Her grin reminded Milly of a beauty queen waving to the crowd in a parade. Her eyes seemed to peer right through her. She didn't know which was scarier- Evie with her unusually good mood or Cora with her obsession with school.

"Hi Evie," Milly said warily before Cora and she made their way into the kitchen, where all her textbooks were sprawled out on the table. "I think I understand fractional division," Cora said proudly. Like Evie, Cora's eyes were hollow. There wasn't the spark Cora usually had.

"Great," Milly said, forcing a smile. Milly was never good at faking a smile but Cora didn't seem to notice.

"Is there a particular topic you wanted to start with, Milly?" Cora said, opening the new book. "The first section is about classifying different forms of life…"

"Whatever you want to start with," Milly replied.

Milly let Cora read aloud from the science book while she pretended to pay close attention. Cora didn't even stop to giggle when she got to the section about animal reproduction. Finally, Milly knew she had to think of a reason to get in the secret room.

"You know, Cora, remember when we went into the secret room? I saw an old textbook in there that we could supplement with!" Milly said brightly.

"We need to concentrate on *this* textbook, Milly," Cora said sternly. "Out of date textbooks will not be helpful. They could have the wrong information and our education could be compromised."

"We could go through the book and circle each wrong fact!" Milly pushed on.

"You're right, that could be a useful exercise," Cora said, changing her mind.

Before long, they found themselves in the secret room again. Milly handed Cora the old chemistry textbook that must have been Lance's when he was younger. "You go first. Circle anything you think is out of date."

Cora accepted the book and sat on a stool with perfect posture. Her back was thankfully towards the potion area. Milly knew she had to be perfectly quiet and efficient in putting together Canine Communication.

After the first step, Milly remembered she had to wait 20 minutes for the next step. Would Cora stay absorbed in the chemistry book long enough for her to finish the recipe? She nervously stared at her watch, willing the minute hand to go faster. It felt like an eternity until she could finish the last steps, but she was astounded that Cora never once looked up from the book the entire time. Milly did not know that kind of focus!

She poured the finished potion in an empty plastic 7-Up bottle that she had managed to keep hidden in her sweatshirt pocket. Milly let another couple of minutes go by until she couldn't suffer the boredom of watching someone read and longer.

"So… find many mistakes?" Milly finally said.

"I found some that I am wondering about… I was thinking of bringing the book to to school and asking our science teacher, but then I thought, we have a chemistry PhD in the house! I'm going to ask Chester," Cora announced.

"Good idea," Milly replied. She could discreetly get Chester's take on the whole situation at the same time, Milly realized.

As they padded up the stairs, Cora looked over at Milly and her eyes were drawn to the 7-Up bottle.

Milly bit her lip and worried that Cora was going to realize what was going on.

"Do you realize how much sugar is in that?" Cora said in disgust.

"Uhh, yeah... I guess I should really stick to water," Milly said in relief.

Chester's door was wide open, so they let themselves in after a little knock.

"Uncle Chester, how are you feeling today?" Cora started. She didn't bother to wait for any kind of response before going on. "I want to ask you some questions about chemistry. I was going through this old text book and I wanted to find out what is still accurate and what has changed since publication. Here, I highlighted some parts that I thought aren't accurate anymore..."

Chester stared at Cora in bewilderment, and then at Milly. While Cora kept on jabbering, Milly took Chester's pad of paper and jotted down a note.

She wrote, "Chester, I'm pretty sure Cora got the 'medicine' from Lance. She's not herself."

Milly discreetly handed Chester the note, and he read it, and urgently motioned for the paper and pen.

Milly read his reply, "This looks like a new and dangerous potion. I detect elements of obedience, manipulation and permanence. This is very bad. You must find the antidote. Look in my journal."

Milly drew in a sharp breath and nodded gravely. Cora had been talking the whole time, but then stopped abruptly. "Uncle Chester, were you even listening?"

Chester grunted and closed his eyes.

"I guess I will just have to bring this in to our science teacher. He's too out of it," Cora sighed. As they turned to leave, Milly stole a glance back at Chester, who opened one eye briefly and nodded.

As soon as they got back downstairs, Milly excused herself to go back home. She got what she needed for the day: the Canine Obedience potion, and a hint from Chester about the antidote.

Milly couldn't wait to pull out the journal in her bedroom. Apparently, there was information about the antidote somewhere in it. There weren't too many entries left that she hadn't read yet and most were dull. After she finished reading the entire journal, she sighed in exasperation. There were absolutely no entries about the antidote! *Is there a page missing?*

***

Milly cuddled up to Angus that night on the couch in the front room. She slumped her head on his big barrel chest. "Angus, are you ready for it? Tomorrow we'll be able to talk to each other again, but this time it's not only fun and games. I'm sending you on a very important mission. It will help save thousands, no, millions of kids. You'll be a hero," whispered Milly. Angus groaned in contentment.

Chapter 20

After a night of crazy dreams, storms had woken Milly up early at 6 am the next morning. The 7-Up bottle was safely on her desk and she urgently un-twisted the top and took down a big gulp. She didn't even notice the wretched taste this time. Hopefully the storms were done by the time the potion worked so she could send Angus out on his mission right away.

For the next hour, Milly lied on her bed listening to the sharp bangs of thunder. A couple were so loud they shook the house, but soon they only sounded like distant drums.

Her stomach felt bubbly, like she could actually feel the potion start to work. *What if Angus doesn't want to help? Or he can't get into the house?* Her plan felt a little far-fetched, but she had to at least try.

"You were up early this morning," came a voice from the floor. Milly peeked over the side of her bed and couldn't help but give a huge smile. No matter what stress was going on, Angus could always make her smile.

"That's because I have a mission today. And I need your help with it, Angus," Milly replied sweetly.

"My help? For real? Cool!" Angus's ears perked up and his tongue was drooping out of the side of his mouth.

Milly pulled out the last letter from Lance and she showed him the return address. "Do you know where this is?"

"1880 Belmont Avenue. St. Paul. Yes, that's just about two miles away. Southwest of us, I believe. Why?" Angus asked curiously.

"I want you to go spy in this house. There's a guy named Lance who lives there, and he is planning to go to schools to give kids a vaccine that will turn them basically into zombies. In this letter he said he already has a schedule written down: which schools, when," Milly explained.

"Oh my. Is this what you have been up to lately, Milly?" Angus asked.

"Yup," Milly said nonchalantly. "So are you up to the task?"

"Oh, for sure, but I wanted to talk to you about something first," Angus answered, suddenly turning solemn.

"What is it?" Milly asked.

"It's about Tommy. Something is different about him. His smell is off, not to mention I don't hear him play video games anymore..." Angus started out.

"I think Tommy already got the potion I was just talking about! And Cora!" Milly blurted out.

"You didn't make him more of that smoothie you had earlier or anything, did you?" Angus looked at Milly with squinty eyes.

"No… why?" Milly gulped.

"Whatever you gave him before has some similarity to what he's giving off right now, and I do not like that smell," Angus asserted.

"I think the guy who made this potion may have used some of the same ingredients," Milly said.

"Why did you give him a potion?" Angus finally hit the question she was dreading.

"It's a potion called 'Permanent Mood Enhancement'," Milly explained. "Remember when we had that talk about Tommy and how we don't get along anymore? I only wanted his friendship back… and I thought that could help."

"That is not the way to go about it," Angus said angrily. "Talk to him. Connect in some new way, like soccer or learn his video games!"

Milly fell silent.

"Well it doesn't even matter anymore. Lance gave him a different one- a worse one," Milly said urgently as she pulled out a GoPro camera. "Angus, we're borrowing Tommy's camera. I'm going to attach it to the top of your head so when you find the schedule, just look at it so it will be saved on video."

"One question. How do I get inside this guy's house?" Angus asked.

Milly bit her bottom lip and tried not to look worried. "Well, that may be an issue. A lot of houses around here have doggy doors or there may be a door cracked open. Try to be creative."

"What if I don't get in? I don't want to let you down!" Angus said thoughtfully.

"Don't worry, buddy. If you can't get in, you can't get in. Just give it a try for me," pleaded Milly. She stroked his head and stared into his chestnut eyes.

"Of course I'll try. Anything for my best friend," Angus said. Milly just smiled.

Milly carefully affixed the GoPro camera to Angus's head. She kissed him on the top of his head and whispered, "You'll do great, Angus. Just be careful out there and look for cars."

Before Angus headed out the door, Milly pushed the record button and could only think to herself, *this is it!*

Chapter 21

This. Is. Torture. What if he gets hit by a car? What if Lance is at home and catches Angus? Hopefully he likes dogs. He must like them more than kids. Milly thought to herself as she sat on the couch at the front window, hugging her legs. She doubted her plan. She would feel dreadful if anything were to happen to her dog. She could never forgive herself.

One hour later, there was a scratch at the door. She peeked through the window and saw her dog's furry, handsome face. His eyes looked happy. Milly exhaled in exaggeration. She swung the door open and exclaimed, "Well?"

"I got in, and better yet, no one was home! The house had a doggy door in the back. I think it is meant for smaller dogs or cats but I squeezed in! You should've seen me- I almost got stuck halfway through," Angus said giddily.

"Good boy! You are so awesome!" Milly squealed.

"His desk was off of the kitchen. There was a big calendar on it that I think had the schools listed that you were talking about. Hopefully it's all on camera," Angus said.

That reminded Milly to end the recording session and remove the camera. "Let's see!"

Milly brought the GoPro to the computer and started to upload the content. After those long minutes of staring at the computer, willing the status bar to go quicker, Milly finally started the video.

The video started with Angus's sprint down the sidewalk. The bobbing around made Milly feel queasy, but after a couple of minutes the speed slowed to a trot.

"I was a little excited," Angus said sheepishly. "I didn't last too long at that pace."

Milly laughed wildly when the video came to the doggy door in the back of the house. It was probably a good minute where the camera shook around as he had been wiggling through and you could hear Angus muttering, "Of all the stupid things!"

"Don't laugh!" pleaded Angus.

"Sorry, buddy! You were a superstar though!" Milly said, patting his head. Angus looked pleased at this.

The camera panned around the kitchen and when it fixed on the calendar, Milly paused the video. She took a quick screen shot and saved it.

"September 5th, Martin Cove Middle School: 8:30 am; Jackson Elementary 1:30 pm. August 26th, Prescott Middle School: 8:30 am; Bates Hill Elementary 1:30 pm..." Milly murmured aloud. "Oh my gosh! He's going to my school first!" Milly screeched. Things all of a sudden felt that much more imminent.

"Anyways, his schedule is two schools per day and the calendar goes more than three months! There must be over a hundred schools here. He really is planned out," Angus explained.

Angus, I couldn't have done this without you!" Milly said.

"Sure. But what's the next step?" Angus wondered.

"Uhhh, I have to figure out the antidote. We needed to get over this hump first," Milly said, slumping her shoulders. "Any ideas?"

"I saw where the potion must have been," Angus said casually.

"Why didn't you say so?!" Milly cried out.

"I just did," Angus shrugged. Milly clicked on the "play" button again on the computer. After Angus had lingered on the calendar, the video went on to show him exploring the house. After a couple bedrooms and bathrooms, the camera shakily lumbered down to the basement. The basement was dark and creepy. The camera stopped at a workbench with all sizes of glass beakers and measuring cups. The camera came to the end of the workbench. On the cement floor was a huge barrel. All of a sudden the video sprang up and pointed down inside the barrel. Inside, were gallons upon gallons of a clear liquid inside. Angus's sniffing was frantic on the video.

"It smelled like a person who is too cool for jokes and hates animals and kids," Angus sneered as Milly continued to watch in awe.

"I'm not familiar with that smell," said Milly. "But they always say dogs can smell fear. Can you smell other traits?"

"Oh, we can smell everything," Angus bragged. "It's true we smell fear, but we also can tell who is genuine, who is fake, who is conniving, or who wants the world to be a better place. Anyways, that liquid smelled exactly like what Tommy smells like now," Angus went on.

"No surprise there, I guess," Milly said sadly.

"Since you seem to have a great sixth sense, what do you know about cats, Angus?" Milly wondered.

"They get a bad rep. I know they can be indifferent, but they do love their humans. You also may be surprised to know that they are always listening."

"I can see that. Patty told Chester that we were doing the 'Dream Manipulation' recipe," Milly said.

"Oh, I'm sure Patty told Chester even more than that," Angus drawled.

"I think I need to take a break from this" sighed Milly. Her brain was firing so many disorganized, incoherent thoughts. When she got like this at school, or while working on homework, she knew she needed to take a break: play some soccer, swing on swings, or just plain run. The two of them did just that.

Chapter 22

Late afternoon that same day, Milly and Angus were lounging in Milly's room. The potion was due to wear off within an hour and Milly was already starting to feel sad about it.

"Did you have fun today, Angus?" Milly asked.

"Of course! I always have fun with you! But you are kind of procrastinating, hate to bring it up," Angus said, giving Milly a serious look.

"The antidote. Yes," Milly sighed. She grasped the journal and let the pages swing open like an accordion. All of a sudden, she noticed a very slim envelope taped to the back cover. She had never noticed it before because the coloring was perfectly blended together with the notebook.

The envelope was discouragingly thin but Milly carefully peeled it free from the notebook and feverishly opened it.

August 2005

ANTIDOTE

In good conscience, an antidote was created, especially given my suspicions with Lance. There is a vial of super concentrated serum that will erase all effects of any of my potions. This serum can be added directly to a potion, effectively transforming the potion into a harmless saline solution. Also, the serum works after the fact. Only one drop is needed on a person's tongue to negate the potion. I have hidden the vial in the south floorboard in the turret. There is a very small compartment that you can pry open. I am hoping this serum will never even have to be used, but I know it must be available.

Milly's heart began racing. There was an antidote! Milly turned to look on the back. Scribbled in barely legible handwriting looked to be random notes. She stuffed the note into her pocket.

"That's good news, right?" Angus said excitedly. "You can set up your own booth at school and give each kid the antidote right after the shot!"

"Yes, good news! But, Lance will not want anyone fishy around. I say that's the last resort. Really, we shouldn't even let Lance get to that point," Milly pointed out.

"How do you suppose you will stop Lance from getting to that point?" Angus asked glumly.

"I don't know," admitted Milly.

"You should probably at least get the serum so you know you have it... and so you can give it to Cora, Tommy, and Evie right now," Angus offered.

"You're right, but how am I going to get invited over there when all she wants to do is study?" Milly wondered.

"Ask her for math help!" Angus said excitedly.

"Good idea, though I reaallllly don't want to sit through that!" Milly whined.

When Milly called Cora's house, Cora told Milly she was in the middle of writing out a research paper, but Milly could make an "appointment" for the following morning.

"Suck it up, Buttercup!" Angus whispered. "Make that appointment!"

Milly rolled her eyes, but the two girls decided on 8 am the next morning. 9:00 am was already devoted to a presentation on the outline of her research paper to her mom. Milly set the phone down after the call and Angus rolled on his back laughing.

"Angus! Not funny!" Milly said, but couldn't help herself and joined his laughter.

***

Cora didn't even smile when she opened up the front door.

"How was your research paper? Are you ready for the big presentation?" Milly asked in obvious sarcasm.

Not picking up on the sarcasm, Cora replied, "I was up late but I think I'm getting there. If we have time, I could practice on you."

"What's it on?" Milly was genuinely curious at that point.

"Battles of the American Revolution," Cora stated.

"Sounds thrilling," Milly said in a melodramatic voice. Cora nodded back.

Cora led the two up to her room. The math book was already opened to the section on fractional division.

"This is good practice for me. They say it helps you learn by teaching others," Cora said.

Cora started her lesson. She found herself nodding to Cora to feign attention as she felt the mini flat head screwdriver in her pocket. She somehow needed to get to that turret and pry open the compartment to find the serum.

There was some banging coming from the kitchen downstairs, and Cora all of a sudden popped up her head. "Can you hold on for two minutes? That is probably my father about to leave for work and I promised him I would give him a mini-presentation on my paper. It will be quick." Before Milly could respond Cora was already on her way downstairs.

Milly couldn't believe her luck, but knew she had to be fast. She bounded cat-like up to the turret.

"This is the south side," Milly whispered to herself confidently after collecting her orientation. Patty had followed her in and studied her every move. Milly dropped to all fours and scanned the baseboards carefully. There were so many grooves it was tricky to determine which could be the real compartment. Finally, after what felt like too long, Milly noticed one groove that was deeper than the rest. She reached for the screwdriver and pried it open on her first try, popping the compartment door open.

There was a perfect little space that would have fit a bottle the size of nail polish, but it was bare. Milly felt a rush of disappointment wave through her body. *Where is the antidote?*

Patty looked irritated and meowed at Milly expectantly.

"I think you do know what's up, don't you? Do you know where the antidote is?" Milly whispered to Patty.

Patty gave no reply. Milly tiptoed back down to Cora's room and waited for her friend to get back.

"My dad thinks my paper will be 'A' material," Cora proudly proclaimed as she entered the bedroom. Milly smiled weakly in reply.

Milly now felt like it was pointless to be there still and couldn't wait until her "appointment" was up. What she really wanted to do was shake the potion out of her friend, but for now she kept up the act so she could maintain access to the secret room.

***

Milly pushed the peas around her plate and stared at the meatloaf. She loved meatloaf but her brain felt like it was going at warp speed through the thickest of jungles. She wanted to work out the problem but everything was too jumbled. What should she do? Go to the police and hope they listen? Should she go on convincing Lance in letters that this wasn't the right thing to do? She didn't have that kind of time anymore. School was starting soon.

"What's wrong, Milly?" Milly's mom asked thoughtfully.

"I'm just tired," lied Milly.

"Drink some more water," Milly's dad offered.

Chapter 23

On the Sunday morning of Labor Day weekend, Milly was helping her mom bake cookies, but her mind was working diligently trying to figure out a solution to the antidote problem.

"We can put these cookies in your lunch on Tuesday!" chirped Milly's mom.

Milly pulled in a breath. That was a rude reminder that school was starting on Tuesday, and therefore Lance Endicott was preparing to give vaccinations to ALL of her classmates, including her, in two days.

She stared wearily at the calendar where "SCHOOL" was written in fancy block letters on

Tuesday. Milly remembered excitedly adding it on a hot July day when her new school had sent out the school supplies list. Then, she noticed "Dr. E follow-up- Tommy" scribbled in her mom's handwriting on that Tuesday as well. Since Tommy was the "test subject" Milly realized he probably wanted to make sure he had the desired results. She wondered when Cora's follow-up would be.

The phone rang and Milly glanced at the caller ID and saw it was Cora's house.

"Hello?" asked Milly warily.

"Would you like to come over so I can present my research paper?" Cora said.

"Sure I can come hang out, right mom?" Milly calmly replied and glanced at her mom who nodded in response.

"I'll come over in 10 minutes. We have fresh cookies baking!" Milly hung up the phone.

After the cookies were done, Milly's mom insisted on sending a dozen with Milly.

"Save the cookies, I have cut out extra sugars and fats," Cora stated, eying the cookies.

"Good mooooooorniiiiing," sang Evie jubilantly, decked out in fluorescent running gear. Before Milly or Cora could even say a word back, Evie had already started a bouncy run down the sidewalk, her ponytail swaying wildly back and forth.

"That girl really has her health in mind," Cora said in appreciation. Milly rolled her eyes and followed Cora inside. She trudged up slowly, not quite ready to listen to a research presentation.

"School starts in two days," Cora said, her eyes lighting up ever so slightly for the first time since getting Lance's shot.

"Yes, I'm all too aware," Milly replied stoically. Milly wished she could be excited for school like she usually was, but that wasn't happening. She had to figure out how to stop Lance, and time was running out.

"You can sit here," Cora motioned to her desk chair. Milly took a seat and stared expectantly at Cora. Cora didn't waste any time and started her presentation. "First of all, thank you for taking the time to listen to my presentation. The title of my paper is 'The American Revolution: the Battles'. Now before we go into each battle, I wanted to..." Milly already tuned her out and was absently flipping through a kid's version of the National Geographic magazine. She read an article about the whales you can see on a whale watching tour out of Maine. She read about dogs who saved lives. Then, she came to some beautiful pictures of capuchin monkeys, and she stopped to admire them.

Monkeys... wild and crazy monkeys... kinda like me. Milly thought to herself slowly. *That's it! Tommy goes in to see Lance on Tuesday. What if I slip him the Human-Animal Conversion potion and he becomes a monkey or something? Then Lance would think his vaccinations had a bad side effect! There's no way he'd be OK with kids becoming wild, crazy monkeys!*

"I said, what did you think? No matter if it's criticisms, or if you loved it, I want the honest truth," Cora said, snapping Milly back.

"Oh. Um. It was very informative. I like how you explained each battle. In great detail," Milly said vaguely.

"Were you even listening? If *I* can tell you were in the clouds, our teachers will for surely notice," Cora said, crossing her arms.

"I was listening! Really!" Milly lied.

"OK, so what was important about The Battle of Saratoga?" Cora demanded.

"It was the first battle?" Milly offered weakly.

"Wrong! That was the first major American victory. I hope you listen to the *teachers* better," Cora said in exasperation.

"You know what? I'm more interested in science. Can we go in the secret room and study Chester's chemistry notes?" Milly said. If she could get back in that secret room she could put together that monkey potion and give it to Tommy.

"No, Milly, my mom would not approve of that. I told her about the secret room and she has forbidden me to go back in and I agree with her anyway. What's in that room is not our business. On a related note, once school starts I don't think we should be friends. I don't want the teachers to get the wrong impression of me- that I'm not serious about school.

I saw how you paid attention to *me*," Cora said gravely.

The words stung even though Milly knew deep down it wasn't coming from the true Cora. Could they still be friends once Cora gets turned back? *If she gets turned back?*

"I'm sad to hear that, Cora," Milly said, her voice wavering. She held back the stinging tears that threatened to roll out.

"We'll see. Maybe you can earn back my friendship if I see you being a good student," Cora said snobbishly.

Milly turned her mind back to the secret room and the potion she wanted to put together. How was she going to get in there without Cora or anyone in her family seeing her?

As Cora saw Milly out the front door, Milly offered out a last ditch effort. "Can I come over tomorrow and you can help me with an outline for my research paper?"

"Oh? What's the topic?" Cora asked in genuine interest.

"The invention of the vaccine," Milly blurted out. She couldn't think of anything else and "vaccines" were on her mind.

"You have your work cut out for you! Well, tomorrow morning I have my follow-up with my doctor, but maybe in the afternoon," Cora responded.

"OK," Milly said as she was out the door.

***

As Milly's mom made dinner, Milly noticed Tommy at his desk in his room. She realized she hadn't heard the familiar video game music since the "vaccine". She almost missed it. Tommy had three different text books open on his desk and he was busily tapping a pencil against the wooden desk.

He looked up and noticed Milly staring. "Can I help you?" he asked in a hollow, robotic voice.

"Whatcha' reading, nerd?" Milly asked as childishly as she could, trying to draw out some real reaction from her brother, to show he was in that body somewhere. A mean Tommy was better than this robot.

"I emailed each of my teachers to find out what they anticipate we *won't* get to this school year so I can learn it on my own. If all of the students in my class were as diligent and serious as me, I wouldn't have to worry about what we *won't* get to," Tommy said stoically.

"You never know, you might get your way," Milly said sadly, and she turned to leave.

Just as Milly got to her bedroom, the phone rang. Not expecting any phone calls, Milly let someone else in her family answer.

"Milly! It's for you!" Milly's dad shouted from downstairs.

Cora? Milly wondered hopefully. Milly picked up the receiver and said, "Hello?"

"Milly. This is Mrs. Nelson. I wanted to talk to you about something," the voice said from the other end.

"Oh!" Milly said nervously in reply. She was surprised to get a call from Cora's mom.

"Cora is not her herself. She's not doing anything wrong, really, but she's just… different. Do you know of anything going on?" Mrs. Nelson implored.

Milly froze, trying to think of how to respond. She didn't want to give her the whole story right then. "I don't know. She was a little weird today but I don't know why," Milly lied.

"I didn't *think* you would. Just had to check," Cora's mom said sadly.

"If I can think of anything I'll let you know," Milly offered.

"Thanks, Milly. Have a nice night."

"Thanks. Bye," Milly said, hanging up the phone.

Milly needed to get Cora better. She wanted her friend back and Cora's mom wanted her daughter back.

Chapter 24

Milly and Angus were camped out at the front window watching Cora's house and she had already witnessed Cora's dad head off somewhere. It was 8 am sharp on Labor Day. It occurred to her that Lance *must* have the antidote. He wouldn't be that stupid to leave it behind. Did he have the recipe for it too?

Only a couple minutes later, Cora's front door swung open and Milly perked up. Out popped Evie in her running clothes, a bright headband, headphones, and an iPod. It took Milly a few moments for it to register that once Cora and her mom left for the appointment, there would be an empty house, except for Chester of course.

A long 15 minutes later, Milly finally saw Cora and her mom set out in the minivan. *How long are Evie's runs? Do I have time?* Milly sweated nervously and looked at her watch. It was 8:17. She would do her best to be out of there by 8:30, just in case. She figured Evie would be gone for at least half an hour, though, as she remembered Evie bragging about how half an hour runs were nothing to her.

Milly bolted out of her house and when she came up to Cora's front door, she took a deep breath to gather her confidence. Milly turned the knob hopefully, but it wouldn't budge.

Great! No what?! Where do people normally hide keys? Milly looked around at her surroundings, urging her brain to think. She flipped up the doormat, but it was bare. She tilted up each of the decorative potted plants that were on either side of the door. Nothing. She looked at her watch. 8:20.

She ran around to the deck at the back of the house and immediately checked the back door. It too was locked. She looked up and could see that there was an open window on the second floor. She eyed the grill and pushed it up against the house. Milly hopped on top of the grill like a monkey, then hoisted herself up. She was now on top of the small part of the roof that was right above a bay window near the kitchen. The screen on the window was very flimsy and had a gap between the window frame. Milly pried it open easily and hopped right inside the house. She found herself in Cora's room and she felt a pang of sadness and urgency. Her watch now read 8:23. Milly popped her head in Chester's room, but he was sound asleep.

She scampered down the stairs and raced to the secret room and mumbled out "Never grow too old or too serious to play". She couldn't help but think of how Lance took to the extreme opposite of Chester's pledge.

She pulled the metal chain for light and fumbled though the pages, hunting for the animal conversion recipe. She picked it out pretty quickly and read it hungrily.

March 1974
Potion for Human-Animal Transformation
2 servings
5th Draft

2 1/3 cups liquid yuntin
¼ cup powdered rifane
1 tsp horbust
1 pinch dorweigh

Pour rifane and yuntin into a beaker and mix until it is thoroughly combined, stirring about two minutes. Add the horbust slowly and spread out evenly and don't mix together until after you also add the dorweigh. Stir for about one minute and now let the mixture sit at least two hours, but not to exceed three days. The longer the mixture sits, the firmer it gets. The limit is about the consistency of a gummy bear. Results in two minutes and last roughly half an hour. When ready to eat, you must stare at the animal you wish *to transform into. In a pinch, a picture is adequate.*

She looked at her watch. 8:25. The stirring and waiting alone would take three minutes! She set out to work right away, determined not to waste a single extra second.

Her hands shook as she tried not to spill the horbust. Finally, she was able to stir the concoction after she added the last ingredient, dorweigh. She tried to calm her nerves with the rhythmic and deliberate stirring. She stared at her watch as the minute hand ticked to 8:28. She hurriedly covered the beaker in cling wrap that had still been sitting on the work counter and she exited the secret room. Did she remember to turn off the light? No time to check!

Gripping the beaker, she bolted upstairs to make her escape. She got to Cora's room and was about to exit the window when she heard the door from downstairs creek open.

"Fa, a long, long way to ruuuuuuun! So, a needle pulling thread! La, a note to follow so! Ti, a drink with jam and bread…" Evie belted out exuberantly.

Milly smirked to herself, but then snapped herself back to her task. She slipped out the window and she replaced the screen as best she could. Milly placed the beaker on the edge of the roof. She lowered herself slowly until her toes felt the grill underneath. She then stood on her tiptoes on the grill and strained to reach the beaker. When she secured it, she landed squarely on the deck and looked around for any witnesses. *Evie was oblivious: check. No nosy neighbors: check.*

Satisfied, she walked back to her house, containing her urge to run. Though she had the animal transformation potion, she wished she had more time in that secret room to figure out the antidote.

Milly sat on her bed and let out an exaggerated sigh. The next step was to figure out how to give Tommy the potion at the exact right time for his appointment.

Chapter 24 1/2

As a trained scientist, Lance knew the scientific process and he was especially careful throughout his professional life. He went through years and years of practiced perfection. Today, he verified that the potion worked on the female test subject. His male subject had an appointment on that Tuesday, but Lance only kept the appointment to go through the motions. He would start Operation Obedience of Children the next morning, then dash to the clinic for the male patient's appointment in the afternoon.

The odds were stacked that his potion would do exactly as he intended. He had played around with the potion recipes for years and years, ever since he was introduced to his father's lab. He even had in his possession the antidote, which he would

PROBABLY NEVER EVEN NEED TO USE IN HIS LIFE-TIME.

THE WORLD WOULD REAP THE REWARDS AND COME TO SEE HIM AS A HERO. CHILDREN AS WE KNEW THEM WOULD CEASE TO EXIST- AND IN THEIR PLACE THERE WOULD BE PRODUCTIVE, MINIATURE ADULTS.

Chapter 25

Milly lingered outside the kitchen while her parents were putting together lunch. Their voices sounded serious, so Milly concentrated on hearing their words.

In a hushed voice, Milly's dad said, "The old Tommy has to be in there somewhere. Maybe you should bring up this change in behavior at the doctor follow-up tomorrow."

"Yeah, maybe it has something to do with that bite that Dr. Endicott was worried about. This is so not Tommy," Milly's mom said sadly.

Milly decided to get the ball rolling on edging her way in on Tommy's appointment.

"My throat hurts," Milly moaned convincingly.

"Huh, maybe it's allergies," Milly's mom commented, watching little fluffs out the window dance in the wind.

"Hopefully. I wouldn't want to be sick for the first day of school," she lied.

***

Milly's alarm blared rudely at 7 am sharp. It was Tuesday and it was supposed to be the first day of school. The bus would be outside her front door in half an hour. She sprang out of bed and started wildly doing jumping jacks. She would *not* be getting on that bus, and she would *not* get that shot today. She *was* going with Tommy and her mom to the clinic to slip him the potion gummy, though. Was Lance going to start the "vaccines" that morning at school? She felt queasy in her stomach.

After a good five minutes of jumping jacks, she dove to the floor and counted off 15 push-ups. She easily got a good sweat started, but then she had to wait for her breathing to slow down before she went down to the kitchen. Tommy was already dressed and almost done with his breakfast. He was just finishing his prunes and plain peanuts.

"Constipated," Tommy said nonchalantly. "And I could use the protein and healthy fats."

"Right," Milly replied.

"Milly! You're not dressed yet?" Milly's mom exclaimed.

"I don't feel good," Milly moaned.

Milly's mom felt her damp and warm forehead and sighed, "No school for you, missy."

"You should really set up some sort of online learning that she could do from home today, mother. I would hate for her to already get behind on the first day of school," Tommy said, looking very serious.

Milly couldn't believe she wanted the old Tommy back who would have hurled insults instead of sagely advice.

"Tommy, I'm picking you up from school for your appointment a little after lunch," Milly's mom said, turning toward Tommy. "Right, I do have that in my planner. I am almost certain that tick bite was nothing. I did a lot of research on the topic," Tommy said.

"I-I, well, we're going in just to be sure," Milly's mom said. Milly knew the real reason she wanted to bring Tommy to the doctor.

***

At the kitchen table during lunch, Milly whimpered, "Mom, my throat is even worse. It feels like there are knives slicing me. Every time I swallow I want to cry." She looked up at her mom with the most pathetic, sickly eyes she could muster.

"Oh, sweetie! I wonder if you have strep again! That settles it, I'm bringing you to Dr. E with us," Milly's mom gushed.

"I hate the strep test," Milly whined. She had a show to put on.

"Don't worry Milly, the nurses are very good at getting that swab sample quickly. We'll be in and out. We're leaving after lunch," Milly's mom replied sensitively.

Milly snuck a Ziplock and butter knife and made her way upstairs to her room after lunch and pulled open the drawer where the potion gummy was safely stored. The mixture had turned into a gummy texture. She cut a small portion about the size of a gummy bear, and tore out the page of the magazine that had monkeys on it and folded it neatly. She had the gummy and the "inspiration" tucked in her pockets.

"Let's do this," she whispered to herself.

***

Milly didn't remember the car ride to the school and then on to the clinic ever being as short as it was that afternoon. Traffic seemed to be going in the opposite direction and they got every green light. She didn't feel quite ready to face the doctor, yet would she *ever* really be ready?

The clinic waiting room was quiet except for a baby and a toddler with their dad. While Milly's mom checked in at the reception, Milly debated with herself when to give the gummy to Tommy. If she gave it too soon and Tommy wasn't called back yet, Milly's mom would have to watch her son transform into a monkey. She didn't know if she wanted to put her mom through that, yet that would be better than Milly not getting it to him at all!

Milly dug into her pocket and pulled out the folded picture of the capuchin monkeys and smoothed it flat with her fingers. Would this potion really work? Would there be a monkey bouncing off the walls shortly? Milly hadn't felt this nervous since the first time she tried the Canine Communication potion. They were in the privacy of the secret room during that first experiment. What if a worker seized the monkey and tried to bring him to animal control once Tommy transformed? Or worse yet it didn't even work? Her thoughts sprang to Cora… and to all of her classmates, whether they were her friends or not. She hated to think they would forever be obedient, mindless zombies. Lance had to be stopped. Her plan had to work.

Milly must have been zoning out for too long because all of a sudden a nurse strode in the waiting room and announced, "Tommy?" In horror, Milly looked over at Tommy who sprang to attention and immediately snapped his book on modern architecture shut.

Tommy stood up and Milly saw their mom rush over to the nurse first. As they were in a hushed conversation, Milly saw her opportunity.

"Hey Tommy, wait. This was from a sample that came in the mail. They're health supplements- I guess for fiber. I had one and it wasn't sweet enough for me. Do you want the other?"

"Not now, Milly," hushed Tommy.

"Just have it! It will melt in my pocket," Milly urged him. With that, Tommy popped it in his mouth.

"Isn't this a cute picture of monkeys?" Milly said convincingly, shoving the picture basically up against his nose.

"Yes. Thanks for fiber sample, although I have no idea how it wasn't sweet enough for you. It's basically a gummy bear," Tommy replied, gently pushing the picture away.

Milly watched Tommy follow the nurse to the back area.

"Don't worry, you'll be next," Milly's mom whispered. She gave Milly a reassuring smile.

Sure enough, another nurse entered the waiting room. "Milly?"

Milly folded the monkey picture and shoved it in her pocket. Milly's mom asked, "Do you need me back there?"

"Nah," Milly answered, as she followed the nurse back.

She knew the drill. First height and weight in the hall, then they'd go in a private room where she'd get the battery of questions and the nurse would take her temperature, pulse, and blood pressure. After they entered room 12, the nurse gingerly closed the door.

"So, Milly, what brings you in today?" asked the nurse sweetly.

"My throat is killing me, and I had a fever. I think my mom wants to see if it's strep," Milly replied in a feigned pathetic voice. It felt weird lying to a nurse.

"When did your symptoms start?"

"A couple days ago I felt a little off and yesterday it started getting bad."

"Oh, you go to Martin Cove Middle School now, right?"

"Yeah…" Milly slowly replied. The nurse jotted down some notes.

"I'll need to get you a vaccine you missed, then. There's a new strain of flu that we have to protect you against," the nurse said matter-of-factly. She must have sensed Milly's mood, as she quickly and sweetly cooed, "Don't worry, sweetie, it's like your yearly flu shot. It just stings for a second."

CHAPTER 25 ½

AT THIS POINT, HE JUST NEEDED TO GO THROUGH THE MOTIONS. JOT DOWN OBSERVATIONS. THE OBSERVATIONS THAT PROVE HIS POTION WORKED SEAMLESSLY. TO REASSURE THE PATIENT'S MOTHER, HE WOULD NEED TO TAKE A BLOOD SAMPLE, OF COURSE, WHICH HE WOULD IMMEDIATELY SEND OFF TO BE TESTED FOR TICK DISEASES. HIS WORK IN THE CLINIC TODAY WAS JUST A NECESSARY STEP. AFTER THAT APPOINTMENT, HE WOULD NEED TO GET TO THE NEXT SCHOOL IN HIS PLANNER.

HE CLUTCHED TOMMY HAGEN'S CHART AS HE RAPPED ON THE DOOR. HE BRISKLY OPENED THE DOOR, AND ON AUTOPILOT, HE WORE A FORCED SMILE.

WHAT HE WAS NOT EXPECTING WAS A CREATURE ON TOP OF THE COUNTER OPENING UP THE CONTAINER OF COTTON BALLS. A MONKEY, PROBABLY QUITE DIRTY, WAS WEARING EXAMINATION GLOVES

AND HAD STARTED TASTING THE COTTON BALLS WHEN IT LOOKED AT HIM AND START SCREECHING. IT BOUNCED TO THE EXAMINATION TABLE AND THEN SPRANG AGAIN TOWARDS THE DOOR. HE JOLTED OUT THE DOOR AND SLAMMED IT SHUT. HE HEARD A THUD ON THE OTHER SIDE OF THE DOOR.

"JANICE!" HE THUNDERED.

A NURSE IMMEDIATELY RAN FROM THE NURSE'S STATION AND JOINED HIM OUTSIDE THE EXAMINATION ROOM.

"DR. ENDICOTT?" SHE BREATHLESSLY ANSWERED.

"THERE IS A MONKEY IN THERE. WHERE DID THE PATIENT GO?" HE SPOKE CLEARLY BUT CONDESCENDINGLY.

"WHAT ARE YOU TALKING ABOUT?" THE NURSE STAMMERED. "I JUST TOOK THE BOY'S VITALS. THERE WAS NO MONKEY IN THERE!"

"WELL, THERE'S A MONKEY IN THERE NOW!" HE ROARED. HE DIDN'T KNOW WHY HE WAS TAKING IT OUT ON HIS BEST NURSE. ALL OF A SUDDEN, IT HIT HIM. THIS WAS A DELAYED SIDE EFFECT OF THE POTION. MONKEYS JUST DON'T REPLACE BOYS FOR NO REASON. HOW COULD THE POTION HAVE GONE THIS TERRIBLY WRONG?!

"I DON'T KNOW WHAT TO SAY, DR. E," SHE REPLIED, SHAKING. SHE STARTED TOWARDS THE EXAMINATION ROOM BEFORE LANCE STOPPED HER SUDDENLY.

"GOTCHA," HE SMIRKED.

THE NURSE STRAINED A SMILE AND CHUCKLED. "GOOD ONE, DOC. THANKS FOR SCARING THE DAYLIGHTS OUTTA ME." SHE SIGHED AND MADE HER WAY BACK TO THE NURSE'S STATION.

HE KNEW HOW TO PLAY THIS OFF. NO ONE MUST KNOW ABOUT THIS. HOW MUCH TIME DID HE HAVE BEFORE THE SCHOOL KIDS WOULD BE TURNING INTO MONKEYS? THIS TEST PATIENT TOOK A WEEK FOR THE DELAYED SIDE EFFECT. LOGISTICS OF GETTING THE ANTIDOTE TO ALL THE KIDS STARTED TO SWARM HIS BRAIN. HE WAS SO IRRITATED AT THE WHOLE SCENARIO. IF MONKEYS WEREN'T SO OBNOXIOUS, HE PROBABLY WOULD HAVE JUST LET THE KIDS TURN INTO THEM.

LANCE GATHERED HIMSELF AND INCHED THE DOOR OPEN. HE QUICKLY STEPPED INSIDE AND CLOSED THE DOOR SWIFTLY BEHIND HIM. THE MONKEY JUST LOOKED UP AT HIM WITH BIG CURIOUS EYES.

LANCE PULLED OUT A VIAL FROM HIS FRONT SHIRT POCKET, DREW OUT A MINUSCULE AMOUNT, AND SAID, "OPEN UP, MONKEY." WHEN THE MONKEY WOULDN'T OPEN HIS MOUTH, HE FORCED IT OPEN AND MANAGED TO GET A SINGLE DROP OF ANTIDOTE IN HIS MOUTH. THE MONKEY SHRIEKED IN ANGER AND SWATTED THE DOCTOR'S OTHER HAND THAT WAS HOLDING THE VIAL. THE BOTTLE FELL IN WHAT FELT LIKE SLOW MOTION, SHATTERED ON THE FLOOR, AND THE LIQUID QUICKLY DISPERSED ON THE FLOOR. ALL LANCE COULD DO WAS STARE WIDE-EYED AT

201

THE FLOOR. WHAT ABOUT THE REST OF THE KIDS? HOW WAS HE GOING TO FIX THINGS NOW!?

Chapter 26

Milly sat on the examination table with her legs hanging down, crossed at the ankles. Normally she hated this waiting part, but she dreaded the moment Lance would step in. She gasped when the door opened and he came in. Instincts told her to look down and avoid him as much as possible, but instead she stared into his eyes, challenging him.

If Milly was not mistaken, he looked a little shaken up. "Milly, I hear you have a sore throat."

"Yeah," she said, refusing to let her voice waver. She didn't let her eye contact falter. She had a new confidence from this whole escapade and she liked it.

He went through the usual doctor assessments while Milly kept her face serious. "I'm ordering a rapid strep test and a culture, and then you can be on your way," he said curtly. "My nurse said you need a vaccine but she was mistaken. I will let her know you don't need it."

She held in a big sigh of relief, but inside she wanted to scream with happiness. The gummy potion must have worked on Tommy! She had just outwitted Lance!

***

In the car ride home, Milly just smiled to herself and took in the happenings of the world as it was whizzing by.

"Just because the rapid strep test came back negative doesn't mean you're in the clear, honey, " Milly's mom said, looking at Milly in the rear view mirror.

"I know, but maybe it's just a cold," she said, still smiling.

"Ew, don't get your germs on me, sickie," Tommy sneered. He then snuck their mom's cell phone out of her purse and started noisily playing Tanks.

"Tommy, be nice," Milly could hear her mom order, though in quite a cheerful voice. "Milly, I think we have our Tommy back."

"I think so too," she said softly. She never thought an insult from Tommy would be such music to her ears.

***

Later that afternoon, while Milly was hanging out in her room pondering the day's events and what her next step would be. She was certain she wouldn't have to do anything- that Lance would give everyone the antidote on his own after the whole monkey episode. Maybe her work was done! She startled when she heard a knock on her door, and Tommy creaked open the door. "I gotta tell you something, Milly," Tommy said seriously.

"What's up?" Milly asked, though she knew what he was probably getting at.

"I-I-I was a monkey at the doctor's. A monkey." he rasped hysterically but quietly. He truly looked disturbed.

"You haven't told mom?" Milly asked warily.

"No, are you kidding? She wouldn't believe me! The only person I could think of that would believe this nonsense was... you!" Tommy urgently whispered. "Why do I have the feeling you knew about this!?"

"Well, it's kind a long story," Milly started. She unleashed the whole story starting from what the real use of the code was. She ended with, "And I didn't tell you any of this because I knew you wouldn't believe me. Or you would've told mom and dad."

"You're right, I would've said you were nuts. But I wouldn't have told mom and dad," he corrected her.

"Really!? Well you brought up the code in front of them at dinner, remember?" Milly said angrily.

"I didn't know it was important," Tommy said. "Milly, there's a problem, though. Right after Dr. E gave me that drop of antidote, I knocked his hand and the whole vial crashed and broke on the floor," Tommy said sheepishly.

"WHAT?! We need that antidote! Cora and her sister need it- and all the kids at our school! What are we going to do now?" Milly exclaimed desperately.

"Sorry, I didn't know what Dr. E was doing- I didn't know it was an antidote! I panicked!" Tommy said. "Is the recipe for the antidote anywhere? It's gotta be!"

"We never saw a recipe for the antidote," Milly started, but then she ran over to her desk and pulled out the antidote note she had saved in her pocket from Cora's house. Her eyes scanned the note as she re-read it, finding nothing particularly helpful. Sighing, she turned the note over and remembered the notes written in chicken-scratch.

Ingredients: govarti, trimpin, my tears. One ounce each of gavotte and trimpin and just three drops of tears. Effective immediately.

Milly stared in disbelief. They could make the antidote themselves!

"What in the heck is govarti and trimpin? And whose tears?!" Tommy exclaimed in disgust.

"Oh, I think I remember seeing those ingredients in the secret room. And apparently Chester's tears?" Milly said, cocking her head to the left, looking up in thought. It was odd that none of those ingredients surprised her at all. "Will you come with me and help?"

Chapter 27

Milly's palms were sweaty when she held the telephone and dialed Cora's number. She was hoping no one would pick up the phone signifying that the coast was clear so she and Tommy could go in the secret room.

"Hello?" chirped Cora's mom from the other end.

"Oh, hi Mrs. Nelson. I was just seeing if I could get something from your house that I need. I-I-I think Cora left me some syllabuses from our first day of school. Can I come get them?" Milly didn't know where those words came from and she certainly didn't know what she would do next if she did get over to their house.

"Cora is very busy and told me to not interrupt her," Cora's mom said.

"I won't bother her. I'll just get them and leave," Milly persisted.

"Oh, alright."

Milly grabbed a tiny Tupperware that was meant for storing small a amount of sauce, and she and Tommy headed over to Cora's house. Milly's mind was racing as they strode across the street. How were they going to get in the secret room when Cora's mom was probably right over her shoulder? All of a sudden, she came up with a plan.

The door swung open and Cora's mom greeted them. "Hello Milly. And this must be Tommy?"

"Angus just ran away! When I opened the door, he bolted without looking back. And my mom just went on an errand!" Milly said as panicked as she could muster.

"Oh no, dear! Did your mom bring her cell phone? I could try calling her," Cora's mom said.

Milly hadn't thought of that. She quickly answered, "Oh, she never brings her cell phone on errands. I don't know, she's weird." *How dumb did that sound? No way will she buy it.*

"OK, how about this? I can get in my car and try to track him down, and after you get the syllabuses from Cora- she's in her room- you can head back to your house in case he comes back on his own," Cora's mom said urgently. She trotted to the kitchen and jotted down on a scrap piece of paper. "Here's my cell, call me if he comes back." Milly took the paper and felt a wave of utter happiness. She couldn't let that show through, though!

"Thank you so much, Mrs. Nelson," Milly said, trying to squeeze out some tears. She managed to get her eyes watery enough.

Milly motioned for Tommy to follow her up to Cora's room as Cora's mom collected her essentials and was out the door. Halfway up the staircase, Milly paused and listened for the front door to close, then led them back down.

"You ready for this?" Milly asked Tommy dramatically.

Tommy just grinned in reply.

"Never grow too old or too serious to play!" Milly exclaimed. Tommy gave her an odd side glance.

The bookcase creaked open and revealed the secret room. Milly felt a new excitement going in with Tommy, and she was proud in a way. She stared into his face to gauge his reaction.

"Cooooooool!" Tommy said in awe.

Milly wished she could show him around- show him all the different recipes for everything, but she felt an urgency to get going on the antidote. She fished out the antidote recipe from her pocket and started scanning the bottles to find govarti and trimpin. Meanwhile, Tommy was slowly letting his eyes wander around the whole room. He was speechless and mesmerized.

"I have definitely underestimated you, Milly," Tommy finally said.

"Yeah, I know," Milly smirked.

She showed him govarti and trimpin in her hands. Govarti was a pale blue; it looked kind of like mouthwash. Trimpin was clear but seemed thicker, like the consistency of cream.

She pulled out the small Tupperware that she would use to hold all the ingredients together. As opposed to all the other recipes that were very specific, this recipe was very minimal. She decided that to be safe, she should probably get the tears first, since that would be the biggest challenge. She handed Tommy the govarti and trimpin.

"You hold on to these. C'mon, we need to go to Chester's room. Follow me," Milly said in her newfound authority.

"That's it!? We spent, like, two minutes in here. I want to explore!" Tommy argued.

"We have to be quick! Come on!" Milly persuaded him. Tommy stuffed the govarti and trimpin in his pocket and followed Milly out of the secret room, pouting.

She started to get very nervous as she padded up the stairs. Cora's bedroom door was closed. She led

Tommy on to Chester's room and she delicately rapped on his open door.

"Hello Chester, sorry to bother you!" Milly said. She grabbed Tommy's hand, while he tried to protest by standing firmly outside the door. He finally relented and followed her. It felt comforting to have Tommy by her side even though he was more scared than she was.

"Chester, we need your help. This is Tommy, my brother, by the way," Milly began. She started on the recent happenings. She didn't want to admit that she and Cora gave Evie and Tommy the Permanent Mood Enhancement or that the one known vial of antidote had been destroyed, but it was too important to the situation. At the end of her long-winded explanation, she casually mentioned, "Cora and Evie- plus hundreds of kids from our school need the antidote as soon as possible! And I need your tears!" She pulled out the antidote recipe and handed it to Chester. "This is your handwriting, right? I need *your* tears?"

Chester stared at Milly and Tommy as he held the note in his knobby fingers. His eyes looked worried.

He motioned for his notepad and pen, which Milly got for him instantly.

His message said "I know about everything. Patty has been keeping me informed. Please make the antidote."

"Oh, wow! Did you make a *permanent* Feline Communication or something?" Milly asked. She wasn't surprised after watching the two of them together. Chester slowly nodded his head and grinned.

Milly was impressed he could talk with cats, but it dawned on her that Chester knew and hadn't even been trying to fix anything. Milly didn't want to be rude, but she gently asked, "Were you going to do *anything* about Lance's plan!?"

He got a sad look on his face, and managed to choke out some garbled words. "I didn't think Lance would really go through with it."

"You risked it all on a hunch? Why *wouldn't* he go through with it? He's a monster!" Milly argued angrily.

"I don't know what to say," he rasped.

She didn't want Chester to feel bad, but she knew he made a mistake. She grasped his hand and squeezed it. She felt she had known him for years now, like he was her own great-uncle. "It's OK, Chester, don't feel-" she began.

Chester interrupted, "I was a coward. Plain and simple. I didn't want to take responsibility for creating the monster that is my son. I introduced him to my experiments and I never let him be a kid. I realized it, but it was too late." Those last words were hardly discernible as his voice was faltering. His face fell into a deep sadness.

Milly quickly pulled up the lid of the Tupperware. She had sensed the tears before they started. She said, "The tears will make up for it. Tommy and I have got the rest covered."

He nodded and let three slow tear drops fall into the Tupperware. He scribbled out another note. "Sorry. And thank you."

Milly squeezed Chester's hand once more, and said, "You're welcome. We're fixing this. But before we go, I need to know something. If the police get involved will you tell them the truth?"

He nodded assuredly, and then closed his eyes in exhaustion. With that, Milly and Tommy scurried downstairs quietly. Angus bellowed as soon as Milly and Tommy went back inside their house. "Thanks Angus, we were pretending you ran away," Milly said casually as she patted his head.

After getting off the phone with Cora's mom who was relieved at the "finding" of Angus, Milly ushered Tommy up to her room. He placed the govarti and trimpin on her desk, and Milly set down the Tupperware of Chester's three tears. "I guess let's just add these and it'll be set!"

She let Tommy add the two, then she closed the lid securely and gave it some quick shakes. "You really seem to know what you're doing," Tommy noted.

"And you thought I was slow," Milly teased, shoving him a little. The blue of govarti faded and the mixture was as clear and as thin as water.

"Well, you couldn't break that easy code," Tommy reminded her with a playful tone. "So, what now?"

Chapter 28

Milly and Tommy stood reluctantly at the bus stop. Their parents were adamant that they needed to go to school that Wednesday morning. The antidote bottle was safely in Milly's pocket, but they didn't have a plan on how they would distribute it to all the kids. Lost in thought, Milly hardly noticed that Cora and Evie had joined them at the bus stop.

"You decided you have time for school today, huh?" Cora said condescendingly.

"Yup," Milly answered, pulling the small Tupperware from the outside pocket of her backpack. "We have something for you two."

Cora didn't answer.

"I just need to put a drop on your tongue," Milly pleaded as she approached Cora.

"No! I feel great. Never better. I feel focused," Cora argued.

"This will make you feel **even** better," Milly said, taking another step towards Cora.

"No, thank you," Cora said sternly.

"Chester knows everything and not only because I told him! He's been talking to Patty. He wants us to fix things!" Milly blurted out.

"Oh, right. Chester can barely even write out 'Please bring me water'," Cora sneered. "It would benefit you if you started taking real things seriously. Like your education and preparing to be a productive adult."

The school bus lumbered from around the corner and approached them. Milly quickly stuffed the Tupperware back into her backpack. *This is going to be harder than I thought.*

Cora and Evie stepped up into the bus, and Milly and Tommy followed reluctantly. All the front seats were taken, which was unusual, so Milly and Tommy sat together in the middle of the bus.

"How are we going to get everyone to take the antidote? There's no way! If they wouldn't take it, no one will," Tommy rasped urgently.

"I don't know!" was all Milly could reply back. The rest of the ride, Milly and Tommy sat together in silence. The bus was eerily quiet. Milly had never been on a bus that quiet before. Usually there was at least talking. Milly looked at the driver curiously. *What did he think of this new quiet? Was he happy?* The driver just stared ahead and gave no inclination he thought things were off.

Milly stood up at the next bus stop just to check out all the kids. All of them, every single one, were sitting upright with perfect posture and staring absently at the seat in front of them.

Across the row, she noticed Elsa, a classmate she was at least kind of friends with in the past, and smiled at her. Elsa held eye contact with Milly but did not smile back.

"How was your summer?" Milly asked hopefully.

"No talking on the bus. It distracts the driver," Elsa rasped back.

Milly sighed and sat back down. Tommy looked genuinely scared.

***

Milly's homeroom teacher was Mrs. Johanson. Every kid in class was sitting at their desks in perfect silence, and had the same perfect posture she had seen on the bus. Cora was in the front row and had her notebook opened. She was staring at the teacher expectantly.

"Good morning, class!" Mrs. Johanson chirped cheerfully. After a few moments, she added, "That's when you say 'Good morning, Mrs. Johanson' back." She smiled and winked to show she was half-kidding.

"Good morning, Mrs. Johanson," the entire class except Milly said dully in unison. Milly looked around and noticed not one of the kids smiled.

Although Mrs. Johanson looked taken aback, she went on, "Yesterday was hectic, being the first day of school and the interruption of the vaccine. In fact, the whole first week of class is overwhelming. We need to take some time to get used to the new schedule and to make sure we all get to know each other."

No one made a single peep. Mrs. Johanson nervously drummed her fingers together. "We have one student who missed the first day. Please introduce yourself to the class and say one thing you did over the summer," Mrs. Johanson said, looking and nodding at Milly.

Milly felt the familiar dread of talking in front of the whole class. "My name is Milly. This summer I went to the park a bunch with Cora," Milly said nervously, pointing out her friend.

Cora's eyes flashed angrily and she shifted her vision to the teacher, ignoring Milly's gaze.

"Wonderful!" Mrs. Johanson said smiling.

A boy shot his hand up, and Mrs. Johanson said, "Yes, Marco?"

"Now that we have that out of the way, I suggest we get started with math," Marco said in a very adult-sounding tone.

"I thought we'd play a game where we get to know each other. You each will go around the room and find out what kinds of pets all of your class-mates have. Then you will make a graph and find out the most popular pets," Mrs. Johanson announced. A girl's hand shot up. "Yes, Amanda?"

"Pardon me, but isn't that a bit… juvenile?" Amanda stated. "What about math?

"It-it-it is math related; we're making graphs," Mrs. Johanson said, surprised. "What's gotten into you all?"

No one answered, but Milly saw all the students stand up and start going around to each other mur-muring questions about each others' pets. Cora went up to Milly but didn't even look at her. "What pets do you have?" Cora asked plainly.

"Cora, you *know* I have one dog. Angus. Remem-ber?" Milly said, aghast.

"Oh, it's you," Cora said looking at Milly again. "So one dog. Thanks." Cora was about to move on, but Milly grabbed her arm.

"Please let me give you a drop of the antidote. After class?" Milly whispered earnestly.

"No, thank you. And please don't include me in any of your future introductions or what have you. I need to make a good impression," Cora said, staring deeply with her vacant eyes.

Milly exhaled in frustration, and went on finding out her other classmates' pets.

***

Lunch used to be a crazy and loud part of the school day. Milly would always find a trusty acquaintance to sit next to, but when she entered the lunchroom that day, it was dead silent. She looked around, and most of the kids even had textbooks opened up in front of them. Milly took a seat next to Elsa, who didn't even look up.

"Hey," Milly greeted her, but expected nothing in return.

Elsa looked up, nodded, and focused her eyes back on her textbook.

"Whatcha' reading?" Milly asked, searching for some kind of kid in there somewhere.

Elsa put one finger to her mouth and whispered, "Shh."

Milly felt the antidote in her pocket. Part of her wanted to try to get a drop on Elsa's tongue, but she didn't want to arouse suspicion or get in trouble.

All of a sudden, Milly heard laughter and she tried to locate the source in excitement. She quickly realized it was only the adult lunch monitors laughing with each other. *Don't they notice anything? They have to realize something is terribly wrong!* Milly wondered.

Recess was just as creepy as lunch. The only movement Milly noticed was some of the kids jogging laps around the playground. Very deliberate and repetitive. Not one kid was on the monkey bars. Or going down a slide. No one was getting in trouble.

If Milly's wasn't sure about the evilness of the plot before, she was now completely horrified. This was not a world to live in. No kids' laughter. No joy.

Back in homeroom at the end of the day, Milly noticed Mrs. Johanson in serious discussions with the principal and another teacher. They looked around at the students, like they were examining freaks of nature. *They notice things are weird. But will they do anything about it?*

Milly was relieved when she met Tommy on the bus on the way home, but they both remained stoic and silent the whole way home. Milly guessed that Tommy was just as traumatized as she was.

When Milly and Tommy were back at their house, they sat again in silence in Tommy's room. With all the craziness that was going on, she hadn't stopped to think about how happy she was that Tommy was by her side and she wasn't alone anymore in trying to think up a plan.

"I-I... uh... well... thank you for being here with me, Tommy," Milly said shyly.

"No prob, You're getting kinda cool to hang out with," Tommy started, but then quickly added, "Don't let it get to your head, though."

Chapter 28 ½

Lance stared at himself in his bathroom mirror. What went wrong? By the next week, all the children would turn into monkeys. He did not have the antidote anymore and he never knew the recipe to begin with. He could not fix this. Would the public realize it was from the "flu vaccine"? Would they turn on him? He was not planning on finding out. He was already packing a bag to get out of the country. He needed to get as far away as possible. He had second cousins in Scotland, so he had purchased airplane tickets as soon as he got home from the clinic.

He would watch the mess unfold from the comforts of the countryside and would assess the situation from afar. If he was never suspected, he would make his way back to the country and get back to his lab and figure

OUT A NEW POTION. ON THE OTHER HAND, IF THE AUTHORITIES CAME FOR HIM, HE WOULD CONTINUE TO EVADE THEM AND CREATE A NEW TRAVELING LAB. IN EITHER CASE, HIS QUEST WOULD CONTINUE. HE SMILED AT HIS REFLECTION IN THE MIRROR. SINCE CHILDHOOD, HE HAD BEEN VERY PERSISTENT, AND THIS TRAIT FOLLOWED HIM TO ADULTHOOD. LANCE WAS NOT THAT EASILY DETERRED.

HE LOOKED AT HIS WATCH. HIS FIRST FLIGHT LEFT AT 6:30 PM THAT NIGHT, SO HE HAD TIME FOR A MID-AFTERNOON DINNER BEFORE HEADING TO THE AIRPORT. A LOUD MEOW JOLTED HIM AS THE ORANGE AND WHITE CAT STARED AT HIM FROM THE BATHROOM ENTRANCE.

"HELLO, PATTY. I ASSUME YOU'RE HERE FOR ANOTHER TREAT. DOESN'T CHESTER EVER FEED YOU?"

Chapter 29

Usually after school, Milly would relax with a TV show, but there was no time. "What should we do?" Milly said, as she thought of Cora and Evie and all the other students at their school. How would they get the antidote to them? How would they make sure Chester was caught?

Milly let out a gasp as she looked out the window and Patty was staring at her with big amber eyes.

Milly creaked the door open to let Patty in as Angus shook his tail as fast as Milly had ever seen it go. He sniffed Patty excitedly and looked like he had a real smile on his face, with his ears pulled back the way he did when they put a leash on him for a walk.

"What are you doing here, Patty?" Milly exclaimed.

"Something is attached to her collar, look," Tommy pointed out.

Milly did indeed see a small note that was haphazardly stuffed underneath the collar. "Huh," said Milly. She pulled it out and opened it up.

Scribbled in Chester's handwriting was a message. "Patty told me that Lance is leaving <u>tonight</u> for Scotland. Do what you need to do. Now!"

"Do what you need to do," Milly softly murmured to herself. "Get mom's cell phone, then let's go!" she exclaimed to Tommy. She got Angus ready and when they were all set, she pulled Tommy out the door.

Milly wanted to sprint the whole way to Lance's house at 1880 Belmont Avenue, but she forced herself to slow down, knowing it was a good two miles away.

"Where are we going?!" Tommy finally sputtered a couple minutes into the jog, out of breath.

"Lance's house!" Milly replied, her eyes glued in front of her in determination.

"WHAT!? You think you can confront him? Don't you think we should just tell the police, or even mom and dad at the very least?" Tommy said.

"Well first off, *we* are confronting him, not just me…. And secondly, I don't think there's time to explain this whole thing to mom and dad, or the police for that matter. He's leaving the country! … And soon!… We'll get the police involved once we have him under control… Obviously we have to involve them… if we want Lance in jail," Milly said between big breaths.

"What if he tries to hurt us or something?" Tommy squealed.

"Angus will not let anyone hurt us," Milly said assuredly.

After exactly 18 minutes of jogging, they started to slow down as they approached 1880 Belmont Avenue. Angus started whining anxiously as he sniffed curiously at the house.

"I know, Angus, I know. You have to be our guard dog, now," Milly said, patting Angus's head. She knew that Angus didn't understand her at that moment, but protecting them would come instinctively.

They made their way up to the front door and Milly forced herself to ring the door bell. Her stomach was in knots and she did not want to face Lance again, but it was up to her and Tommy to save Cora, Evie, and all the other kids at school.

On the side of the door, Milly saw some curtains shuffle to the side and some eyes peering through the window.

"I see you, Lance, open up! I want to talk to you!" Milly shouted.

After a few tense moments, the door swung open and Lance stared wordlessly at the three of them. "How can I help you? Are you lost or something?"

"Do you even recognize us? You're our doctor, remember?" Milly questioned.

Suddenly, Lance's eyes flashed a sign of recognition, and he urgently looked up and down the street.

"Fine, come in. Hurry up!" he growled. "The dog stays out there."

"No, he comes with us. We can do this out here if you don't let him in!" Milly said, standing her ground.

"OK, just come in," Lance rasped angrily.

They followed Lance in. Milly felt Angus tense up. He was obviously fully concentrated on Lance. Milly noticed a black wheeled suitcase beside the front door.

"Going somewhere?" Milly mused.

"As a matter of fact, yes, I have vacation plans. Now what do you want?" Lance said.

"I need you to come clean. About the 'medicine' you gave to all the kids at my school. And your plans to give it at all the other schools," Milly demanded, getting straight to the point.

"I have no idea what you're talking about," Lance said sternly.

"Dr. E, you don't remember me turning into a monkey?" Tommy piped in, crossing his arms.

"Oh. That. Well, the flu vaccine must've had a weird side effect this year."

"Baloney. We know *everything*. You had plans to give kids everywhere a 'medicine' that would turn them into brainless, obedient, zombie-children," Milly said. She felt the confidence continue to build in her body. She never felt so self-assured before.

Lance stood there motionless and caught off-guard. His hands started forming anxious fists and his expression turned even sourer. He took half a step towards the trio, but Angus immediately bared his teeth and growled. The hair on Angus's back stood straight up and his tail shot out straight behind him. His whole body was rigid and ready.

Lance immediately backed up a couple steps and held out his hands, palms facing Milly, Tommy and Angus. "Easy, now." Lance said. "You don't know what you're doing. Kids will no longer be a drain to society. They will be good listeners and will be much more prepared to be productive adults. What would I be coming clean about? Trying to help!?" he said angrily. "Kids playing games, kids misbehaving in class, kids acting like monkeys will be a thing of the past. They'll all be mini-adults when I'm through. The world will be..." but he suddenly stopped short. "What is that red light?" he growled, pointing towards Angus.

Milly smirked as she glanced at the mini GoPro camera that she had affixed to Angus's collar.

Tommy's eyes lit up as he realized the whole thing had been taped. He pulled out their mom's cell phone and quickly dialed. "Yes, I need help at 1880 Belmont Avenue. You're going to want to arrest this man in front of me... I can't explain it all, just come quickly."

"Why you..." Lance snarled as he started to go after Tommy. Immediately, Angus lunged and nipped Lance's wrist ever so slightly, and Lance cried out in surprise and tenderly cradled his hand.

"If you think you are helping society, I guess you will have nothing to worry about," Milly said calmly, turning off the GoPro. "I think we got what we needed."

Minutes later, two squad cars with lights and sirens on swerved up to the house. Two police officers from each car got out and made their way up to Lance's house.

***

"Young lady, this is quite the feat you two have achieved," an officer with a tight bun and gentle eyes remarked. Officers Julie and Rick had brought Milly, Tommy, and Angus to the police station after telling their mom to meet them there. The other car had taken Lance in. "I always underestimate you kids."

"Oh, I didn't tell you this part yet. I have the antidote right here in my pocket. Every kid that got the fake 'flu vaccine' needs a drop on their tongue and everything will be cleared up," Milly said, pulling out the antidote from her pocket. She handed it to Officer Julie who stared in amazement at it. "Don't lose it. We *could* make more, but this should be enough for everyone."

Milly nervously looked at the entrance to see if her mom or dad had showed up yet. Milly was worried about their reaction, but she felt relieved that she didn't have to hide anything anymore. Lance had been led to another room, no doubt to be questioned. After the police had viewed the GoPro video, Milly and Tommy were allowed to see it. The footage from the GoPro was basically a full confession.

Finally, Milly and Tommy's parents strode into the police station with anxious expressions on their faces. "Is everything OK?" Milly's mom said desperately.

Officer Julie explained everything as Milly and Tommy watched their parents' reactions out of the corner of their eyes. Milly nudged Tommy and gave him a big smile, and he gave an exaggerated look of relief back to her. Angus was lying lazily between their two seats and yawned dramatically. Milly and Tommy chuckled quietly. "Are we boring you, Angus?" Milly said rubbing behind his ear.

The car ride home was filled with Milly's nonstop chatter. She felt like a popcorn kernel that was *finally* able to pop. Not telling Tommy was one thing, but not telling her mom and dad all of the fun things she and Cora had been up to was quite another. She finally felt that even if she did get in trouble, at least she stopped evil Lance from carrying out his plan.

"Milly, Milly, Milly. I'd ground you, but how could I? You saved the day! But seriously, no more potions!" Milly's mom said, half seriously and half happily.

"I don't even care. Ground me! Kids are meant to get in trouble sometimes," Milly said smiling.

Chapter 30

The next morning, Milly and Tommy joined Cora and Evie at the bus stop. All four stood there awkwardly and silently. Milly knew neither Cora nor Evie had gotten the antidote yet. They had vacant expressions and barely acknowledged Milly and Tommy.

On the bus, Milly sat with Tommy. The bus was still creepy that morning, but Milly was hopeful that it would all be changed back soon.

"When will everyone get the antidote? I can't take anymore of this," Tommy whispered anxiously.

"I hope soon!"

At the entrance to the school, there were a couple of nurses stationed at a table. A police officer was with them and she announced, "Your parents already received the message that there has been a major breech in security and you all need to get this antidote. Line up here, everyone!"

The officer pulled Milly and Tommy aside discreetly. "Milly, Tommy, we are presenting an award to you during the school assembly today," she said winking. "I understand you two don't need the antidote, so you can just make your way to your classrooms."

Milly noticed Cora and Evie being filtered towards the line at the nurse's table. Tommy shot her a sly smile and said "See ya in the gym later."

***

Milly couldn't keep her eyes off the door of her homeroom as she watched fellow students arrive and take their seats. She couldn't wait to see Cora- to see if she was back to her old self. Finally, she spotted Cora. Cora smiled brightly and took the seat beside Milly.

"Hi!" Milly exclaimed.

"Hey!" Cora replied.

Milly couldn't take it any longer. "Do you even know how weird you were? It seemed like you didn't even realize you had gotten the potion! How did you let them give you a shot at the doctor?!"

"I was so scared, but I didn't have a way to escape, really, without causing a big ruckus. After, I wasn't scared anymore but I also felt like I had no personality. I didn't care about anything besides school and making the teachers happy. You felt like a stranger to me! I couldn't have cared less to talk to you!" remarked Cora sadly.

"I *know!*" Milly said.

They were cut off, as Mrs. Johanson announced they were all to head to an assembly. Milly felt butterflies in her stomach and realized she was more nervous about standing up in front of the whole school than she was about confronting Lance.

Almost all of the bleachers were already filled when they entered the gym. The 5th graders were ushered to the bleachers on the bottom section on the far side of the gym. She glanced at all the faces. Some were laughing, some looked nervous and self-conscious, and some pleasantly talking with their friends. She noticed two boys playfully shoving each other. She smiled to herself. Before going through the whole ordeal, all these kids would have been so intimidating, but she realized they were all just kids. They all liked to have fun with their friends, and they all had their own interests. Her interests may not coincide with everyone else's, but she had luckily found Cora.

The principal made some general announcements and some words of school spirit, but then he introduced Officer Julie to the microphone.

"There are two students here today that showed incredible bravery and acted quickly to save many kids. A man named Lance Endicott gave most, if not all of you a 'vaccine' that turned you into basically zombies. This man claims he was a hero, but we all know who the real heroes are. Milly and Tommy Hagen stopped this man and even handed us over enough evidence to arrest him. This Proclamation of Bravery is presented to both of you on behalf of the St. Paul Police Department. Thank you for your actions!"

Milly gathered herself, took a deep breath, and made her way to the front. She saw Tommy coming from higher up in the bleachers. His face was beet red, but he couldn't hide his smile. Milly shook Officer Julie's hand when she got up there and accepted a certificate. Tommy did the same, and they beamed up at all the students who were clapping their hands enthusiastically. Several "whoops" came from across the bleachers. Milly never felt happier.

Later, in the halls on the way back to Mrs. Johanson's room, a swarm of students were crowding around her in excitement. Kids were murmuring praise and shock all around her.

"That was *so cool!*"

"Weren't you scared?!"

"How did you *do* all that?"

Milly wasn't used to all that attention and she shyly tried to answer all the questions. She felt proud but would feel relieved when everything went back to normal again.

Chapter 31

After school that same day, Milly went to Cora's house. Her mom greeted her warmly. "Milly, you darling child, thank you so much for everything."

"I'm just glad I have my friend back now!" Milly said, smiling.

Milly and Cora made their way up to see Chester. Milly knew he must be dying to know the whole story. Cora ran up to him and gushed, "Chester! I'm all better now!"

His eyes lit up and a smile spread across his whole face. "Wonderful, tell me everything," he rasped, forgoing his pen and paper.

Milly explained everything, from how creepy it had been with all the "zombies", to when she and Tommy confronted Lance at his house, to her and Tommy's awards at the assembly.

Chester just smiled with tears welling up. He was too emotional to get out his words, so he wrote down a message. "Bravo! Thank you so much!"

***

"You never got to hear about our clinic visit with Lance," Milly said with a sly smile when they got to Cora's room.

"The monkey part is *genius!* I wanna do that!" Cora said after Milly explained everything.

"Guess what…" Milly said shaking a little baggie with a couple squares of the potioned gummy. She also dug out the picture of monkeys and smacked it down on Cora's desk, grinning.

The five minute wait to turn into a monkey was unbearable. Milly had been curious whether it started with one foot and worked its way up, or whether it happened instantaneously. It turned out it was instantaneous. All of a sudden, two little capuchin monkeys were jumping around Cora's room having the time of their lives.

Cora screeched and swung from the top of her dresser to the four poster bed, swinging around each pole. Milly laughed in her screechy monkey laugh, then tried to quiet herself down, which made herself laugh even harder. Milly couldn't believe how light and free she felt as she and Cora chased each other around the room. This would take playing "Lava" on the playground to a whole new level.

Milly had finally gotten the hang of using her tail when they were suddenly transitioned back to girls. Both Milly and Cora panted as if they had just raced a mile. Their sweat-drenched hair was plastered to their faces, and each time they looked at each other they broke down into hysterics again.

"You had such a cute little monkey face," Cora giggled. "Let's stay monkeys forever!"

"I wish! At least let's make a pact to stay kids for as long as we can," Milly said as she calmed down finally. With that, they interlocked their pinkies in promise, and then as if they had planned it out perfectly, they both started hooting like little capuchins.

Chapter 31 1/2

This was not the end of it. This was merely a minor hiccup in his long term plan to wipe out childhood completely. He would crunch down and figure out where the potion went wrong, but he knew he would be back. At the trial next month, the jury would side with him and he would be a free man. He had no doubt.

Lance could not believe bail was set at a million dollars. He had not murdered anyone. He hadn't set fire to a school, so why was the bail set so high? His eyes bored into the bare cell wall in controlled fury. "Kids shall be kids no longer. Sooner or later."

Chapter 32

It was a month into school and Milly was into the school year groove. She still got to spend a lot of time with Cora since they were in the same home-room. Their friendship continued to thrive and they kept to their promises to stay kids a while longer. They ignored the gossip that surrounded them at lunch, and found time to run around at the play-ground while the weather was still nice. When Milly thought back to when she first saw the moving van in front of the intriguing old house, she never would have guessed what great friends they would become or all the secrets they would find... or that she would have to witness Cora turn into a zombie. Looking back on it felt surreal and unbelievable.

Tommy still had his grumpy teenager moments, but Milly found new ways to connect with him by asking for soccer help and even trying to learn his video game. He was in his element on the soccer field. Although he missed part of summer soccer because he had quit, he decided to join the 7th and 8th grade team at their school. No doubt he would be proud if his little sister followed in his footsteps.

***

"Did you hear Lance got a two year sentence?" Milly said one unseasonably warm November afternoon.

"Yes! That seems way too short!" Cora exclaimed. "Do you think he's working on his potion in jail?"

"Maybe. We might have to send Patty on a top-secret mission," Milly remarked seriously. "Not now, though. Let's just be kids today."

With that, they both sprang up off the wood chips and challenged each other to stay off the hot lava. As Milly raced across the monkey bars, she couldn't help but shudder at the thought that they were so close to losing their childhood forever. All the A+'s in the world wouldn't make up for this.

If you enjoyed MILLY AND THE TALE FROM ACROSS THE STREET, please leave a review on Amazon or wherever you bought the book!

Visit www.wordpress.marthaklopp.com *to stay updated on the next MILLY adventure, UP NORTH, due to come out early 2020.*

Martha Klopp is a native of Duluth, Minnesota, and now lives outside St. Paul. She has four children, a loving husband, and two Labrador Retrievers. In her 4th grade yearbook prediction, Martha proclaimed that she would become an author and live right next to Disney World. Plans changed a little bit when she decided Minnesota is where her heart resides.

Made in the USA
Middletown, DE
21 July 2019